LADY, GO DIE!
A MIKE HAMMER NOVEL

MORE MIKE HAMMER
FROM TITAN BOOKS

Complex 90
Kill Me, Darling
Don't Look Behind You (March 2016)
The Will to Kill (March 2017)

LADY, GO DIE!

A MIKE HAMMER NOVEL

MICKEY SPILLANE
and
MAX ALLAN COLLINS

TITANBOOKS

Lady, Go Die!: A Mike Hammer Novel
Print-edition ISBN: 9781781167588
E-book edition ISBN: 9780857686244

Published by Titan Books
A division of Titan Publishing Group Ltd
144 Southwark St, London SE1 0UP

First edition: April 2013

1 3 5 7 9 10 8 6 4 2

This is a work of fiction. Names, characters, places, and incidents either are the product of the author's imagination or are used fictitiously, and any resemblance to actual persons, living or dead, business establishments, events, or locales is entirely coincidental. The publisher does not have any control over and does not assume any responsibility for author or third-party websites or their content.

Mickey Spillane and Max Allan Collins assert the moral right to be identified as the authors of this work.

A CIP catalogue record for this title is available from the British Library.

Printed and bound by CPI Group (UK) Ltd, Croydon, CR0 4YY

LADY, GO DIE!

A MIKE HAMMER NOVEL

FOR OTTO PENZLER
who came through for Mickey

CO-AUTHOR'S NOTE

A week before his death, Mickey Spillane told his wife Jane, "When I'm gone, there's going to be a treasure hunt around here. Take everything you find and give it to Max—he'll know what to do." I can imagine no greater honor.

Half a dozen substantial Mike Hammer novel manuscripts were found among a wealth of unpublished material. *Lady, Go Die!* constituted perhaps the most exciting find. Initially, I thought the brittle, yellow single-spaced pages were an earlier draft of *The Twisted Thing* (published 1966, but written much earlier), because of the shared small-town setting and a few character names. As I read the manuscript, I realized this was something quite special—the unfinished *second* Mike Hammer novel.

The famous first Hammer, *I, the Jury*, written in 1945 but published in 1947, was presented as a post-war adventure. I have honored that continuity here, although the partial manuscript I worked from (circa 1945 itself) originally contained references to World War Two as ongoing. Why Mickey set *Lady, Go Die!* aside, we can never know. But in my biased opinion, it was a yarn well worth finishing.

M.A.C.

CHAPTER ONE

They were kicking the hell out of the little guy.

Halfway down the alley between two wooden storefront buildings, shadows in the moonlight did an evil dance, three goons circling around a whimpering pile of bones down on the gravel. The big guys seemed to be trying for field goals, their squirming prey pulled in on himself like a barefoot fetus in a ragged t-shirt and frayed dungarees. Blood soaked through the white cotton like irregular polka dots, and moans accelerated into ragged screams whenever a hard-toed shoe put one between the goal posts.

"Mike," Velda whispered, grasping my arm.

Two of the baggy-suit bastards had hats jammed on their skulls, the other one, the biggest, was bare-headed with a butch cut so close to the scalp he might have been bald.

I said a nasty word, took a last drag on the cig and sent it spinning into the deserted street. I slipped out of my sportcoat and handed it to my raven-haired companion, who was frowning at me, though those big beautiful brown eyes stayed wide. I held up a hand to her like a crossing guard, and she just nodded.

"Where *is* the dame?" the bare-headed brute demanded. "We played games long enough, Poochie! You must've seen *something*!"

Like the man said, it was none of my business. I was on a weekend getaway with my lovely secretary, trying to ease the pressure of big city life. Just before ten p.m. we'd arrived in Sidon, eighty miles out on Long Island, a little recreational hamlet in Suffolk County. We left my heap in the hotel lot and were having a nice cool evening stroll along the boardwalk, checking out the two-block business section of a little burg that had already gone to bed.

"You wanna die tonight, Poochie?" the big guy was saying. He had three inches on my six feet, and forty pounds on my one-ninety, and there was fat on him, but muscle, too.

And the hell of it was, I knew the son of a bitch.

"You can die right here, Poochie! We'll drop your sorry butt in a hole in the woods somewhere, no one the wiser."

I let the moonlight frame me in the mouth of the alley as I said, "You haven't changed much, Dekkert. Little fatter."

His bully boy associates froze; one in mid-kick almost lost his balance. That was worth a grin.

"Who is that?" Dekkert asked, turning toward me with that stubbly bullet head like a badly superimposed photo over his bulky body. He'd been handsome once, a real lady killer, before his nose became a nebulous thing that had been broken past resemblance to any standard breathing apparatus.

Once by me.

"I heard you were back in the cop business," I said. "I just didn't know Sidon was the lucky winner. You won the sweepstakes yourself when Pat Chambers didn't get your fat ass tossed in the pokey, for all the graft you took."

"...Hammer?"

I was within a few feet of them now—him and his two cronies, a skinny one whose kicks couldn't have hurt much and a broad-shouldered one with the stupid features of a high school star athlete too dumb to land a college scholarship.

Dekkert moved away from his victim, who was curled up crying. He faced me, close enough that I could smell the onions. "What are *you* doing in Sidon, Hammer?"

"Just a little getaway."

"Come back in a couple of weeks, after the season starts. Show you a good time."

"Like you're showing *that* poor little bastard?"

He thumped my chest with a thick finger.

"This is police business, Hammer. Official interrogation in a missing persons case. Why don't you roll on down the road? Wilcox is a more year-round kind of place than Sidon."

He gave me a gentle shove.

"So long, Hammer."

I laughed. "Police business, huh? Usually interrogations take place at police headquarters. Or is this alley the new Sidon HQ?"

This shove wasn't so gentle.

"So *long*, Hammer."

The right I sent into his pan would have broken that nose if there had been enough cartilage left to matter. But the blow still managed to send ribbons of scarlet streaming from his nostrils and down his surprised expression. My left doubled him over, and then my right and left clasped in prayer to smash him on the back of his fat neck, sending him onto the alley floor in a sprawling belly flop.

I was on his back, rubbing his face in the gravel, when

his two clowns tried to haul me up and off. An elbow in the athlete's balls took the fight right out of him, and a sideways kick into the skinny one sent him careening to hit the alley wall like I tossed a load of kindling there. Skinny boy slid down and sat and thought about his lot in life.

I chuckled to myself, wiping my hands off on the back of Dekkert's suitcoat. The little beaten-up figure down the alley was silent, like a child in its crib sleeping sound. The alley dead-ended in a wooden fence, so he wasn't going anywhere.

Still on his belly, Dekkert was the one doing the whimpering and moaning now, and so were his boys. I took the guns off all three of them, since my rod was in my suitcase, and rained slugs onto the gravel out of three Police Special revolvers before I tossed each of them with one-two-three clunks on the gravel, their cylinders hanging out, near their fallen owners.

The skinny one found his voice. "We're… we're *cops*…"

"Nah. You jokers aren't cops. You're hick rake-off artists."

The guy I'd kicked in the nuts was sitting up, hunkered, hands in his lap like he was taking inventory. He spoke with the quaver of a spanked kid.

"You… you better leave town right *now*, Mister."

"Go to hell. I know my legal rights. Three shifty-looking characters were beating up some helpless joe, and I put a stop to it."

Dekkert had rolled over, but otherwise was not making a move. Bits of gravel were imbedded in his face and his forehead was scratched like a cat got at it. His nose had stopped bleeding but the lower half of his puss was a smear of red mingled with the yellow of puke on his lips.

Just like the last time he screwed with me.

"If you want me," I said, tossing them a friendly wave, "I'll be at the Sidon Arms."

I went over to the small, battered prone figure they had called Poochie. I helped him to his feet, gently, and he whimpered some more, but his round-ish face—a child's not quite formed face—looked up at me, eyes bright with both tears and relief, and made a smile out of puffy, blood-caked lips.

"Thanks, mister. Who... who *are* you?"

"Why, I'm the Lone Ranger, kid. And wait till you get a load of Tonto."

Pulling the trigger had been easy. Living with it had been hard. Crazy rage got replaced with a joyless emptiness. No emotion, no feeling. I felt as dead as the one I'd shot.

I had evened the score for a friend but the cost had been high—a woman I loved was dead, and the bullet that sent the killer to hell had along the way punched a gaping hole in my soul. I tried to fill it with booze, or at least cauterize the damn thing, spending most of my evenings at Joe Mast's joint, trying not to fall off a bar stool and usually failing. But it hadn't worked. Nothing worked.

My best friend in the world, Pat Chambers, was a cop. We had been on the NYPD together, till my hot head got me assigned to a desk where I soon traded in my badge for a private license and a shingle that said, "Hammer Investigating Agency."

I couldn't stay a cop. All those rules and regulations drove me bugs. I had a more direct method for dealing with the bastards that preyed upon society—I just killed their damn asses. Killed them in a way that was nice and legal. Self-defense, it's called, and it catches in the craw of your typical self-righteous judge, but none of them and nobody else could do a damn thing about it. They couldn't even take my license away. Because I knew just how to play it.

Just the same, Pat and I stayed friends, maybe because his scientific approach meshed well with my instinctive style—he was fingerprints and test tubes where I was motives and people. I could do things he couldn't, and he had resources I didn't. Usually private eyes and police are like oil and water, but what began as a convenient way for two different kinds of cops to feed each other information turned into a real and lasting friendship.

So when he showed up on the stool next to me, training his gray-blue eyes on me like benign gun barrels, I said, "What's a nice guy like you doing in a joint like this?"

"Velda is getting worried."

Velda was my secretary, and my right arm. She had been with me since I set up shop and I hadn't made a pass at her yet. But there was something special between us that wasn't just boss and employee.

"Tell her to lay off the mother-hen routine," I said. I poured some whiskey in a glass and then down my throat.

"You need to let it go, Mike. It's ancient history."

"Not even a year, Pat."

"Would you change it? Would you go back and not pull that trigger?"

"No."

"Then it's time to move on."

I knew he was right. But I'd fallen into a goddamn self-pitying rut. Work five days a week, drink five nights a week. And on weekends, drink the whole damn time. Being numb was good. You didn't think so much. But if I kept this up, I'd have a liver that even the medics couldn't recognize as a human organ.

Still, I said, "Blow, Pat. I'm a big boy. I can take care of myself."

"No," Velda said, "you can't."

I hadn't even seen the big, beautiful dark-haired doll settle her lovely fanny onto the other stool beside me. I *must* have been far gone.

"And we're not about to let you crawl in that bottle," she said, "and drown yourself."

I gave them a ragged laugh. Hell's bells—they had me surrounded. I pushed the glass and the whiskey away.

"Okay," I said. "Officially on the wagon. Now. What do you suggest?"

"First," Pat said, "you go home and sleep till you're sober."

"Second," Velda said, "we go off somewhere and rest. Someplace where there are no women and no bad guys."

"That sounds dull as hell."

Pat said, "It'll be good for you. You and Velda take the weekend for some R and R. Someplace out on Long Island, maybe."

Velda said, "What was that little town you and your folks used to go out to? Before the war?"

"Sidon," I said. I'd been there a couple times after the war, too. But not for a year or two. "It'll be dead out there. The season doesn't start for a couple of weeks."

"Right," Velda said. "The weather's beautiful just now, nice and sunny and warm but not hot. The beach, the ocean, it'll be like a dream."

"Instead of this nightmare," Pat said, slapping at my glass, "that you been wrapping yourself up in."

I turned to Velda. "You're going along?"

"Sure," she said easily. "Why not? I got a new two-piece bathing suit I want to try out."

"One of those bikini deals?" I said, getting interested. She nodded.

"Hey, I'm game, baby, but I'll be recuperating, you know? From drink and debauchery and a general state of depression? You'll need to stay right at my bedside."

"Separate rooms, Mike," she said crisply, but she was smiling. "I'll play nursemaid and babysitter, only I require my own separate quarters."

"Might as well take you along instead," I said to Pat, "for all the fun I'll have."

He raised an eyebrow and shrugged.

Velda frowned. "No offense, Pat, but you're staying home. I'm not equipped to handle all the trouble you two could get into."

She looked equipped enough to handle anything from where I sat.

"Now," she was saying, climbing off her stool, "can you stand up, or do we have to escort you?"

I made it onto my own two feet. I may have leaned on them a little. A little more on Velda. She was softer and smelled a lot better.

The little guy could walk, but just barely. Velda had found some old sandals near the mouth of the alley that were apparently Poochie's, lost in the struggle. Anyway, they fit him. He wasn't saying anything, but he could stumble along with me on one side and Velda on the other, each holding onto an arm.

We trooped him through the lobby of the Sidon Arms, the only one of the little town's four lodging options open year-round. The building was wooden and old but clean. The lobby was large enough to accommodate a summer crowd but nothing fancy, strictly pre-war, though I wasn't sure what war. I guessed this hotel stayed open all year largely because of the bar off the lobby, where a high-perched TV was showing wrestling and half a dozen locals were nursing beers, watching whoever was battling Gorgeous George this week pretend to lose.

The cadaverous bald desk clerk in mortician's black reacted with popping eyes and a, "Merciful heavens!" Could hardly blame him—Poochie was a tattered, blood-spattered, black-and-blue wreck.

We had not checked in yet but had a reservation. When I announced our names, the clerk pretended Poochie wasn't between us hanging on like a very loose tooth to precarious gums. Everything was handled efficiently. We signed the book, and were told our rooms were adjacent but without an adjoining door. Everything aboveboard for a single man and woman traveling together.

Finally the clerk said, "What about your, uh, friend?"

"Recognize him?" I asked.

"Yes. That is, uh, Poochie. He's Sidon's resident beach-comber. He has a shack on the water, just outside town."

Poochie showed no signs of any of this registering. He wasn't unconscious, though, and had a goofy, puffy smile going. It widened whenever he looked up at Velda.

"He got hurt," I said, which was all the explanation I was in the mood to give out.

"Oh, dear. *Did* he?"

Cripes, didn't this jerk have eyes?

"Is Doc Moody still in town?" I asked. Moody had been a drinking buddy of my old man's, on our visits to Sidon. And I'd tossed a few back with the doc on my last solo sojourn.

"Why, yes he is. Should I call him?"

"There's an idea." I dug out a five and tossed it to him, the way you would a fish to a seal. "Give the doc my name—he'll remember it—and when he gets here, send him up to my room."

Right now I was praying the good doc would be sober enough to see straight.

"Yes, Mr. Hammer," the clerk said, and reached out a

skinny, bony hand for the telephone.

The Sidon Arms had three floors and no elevator. We walked Poochie slowly up the wide lobby stairs and for the first time since we'd made the trek from the alley, the little guy moaned.

Velda said, "It'll be all right, Poochie. It'll be fine."

My room was 2-A and Velda's was 2-B. The rooms were identical—dresser, wardrobe, a couple chairs, double bed, nightstand, no closet, no bath. That was at the end of the hall. Velda went down there to fill a pitcher with warm water and I set Poochie in the more comfortable of the chairs. It was upholstered and had some padding. While she cleaned him up, I went back down to the lobby. The clerk told me Doc Moody was on his way, and I made my way out to the parking lot behind the hotel and got our luggage and brought it up.

Poochie seemed to be coming into focus as I hauled our bags in.

"I think I better give Poochie my bed," I said, standing next to her as she bent dabbing a washcloth gently onto our guest's battered face. She was in a white blouse and a blue pleated skirt and was the kind of nurse you dreamed to get.

"You can sleep with me in my room, if you like." She flashed me the sweetest smile.

"No kidding?"

"No kidding. You know me, Mike—I don't stand on ceremony. And speaking of ceremonies, there's a justice of the peace in this burg, isn't there? Wonder if he makes house calls like your doctor friend?"

"You're no fun at all," I told her. I leaned in and got our charge's attention. "What was that about, Poochie?"

He smiled. It was like Dopey smiling at Snow White.

"What did Dekkert want with you, Poochie? Why did

those creeps give you the Third Degree and then some?"

He shook his head just a little. "Yellow-haired lady."

"What yellow-haired lady?"

"They say she's gone. I live down the beach."

"Down the beach from the yellow-haired lady?"

A little nod, then a wince at the pain it caused.

I asked, "Who is she?"

"Not nice. Not very nice."

"They think you saw something, because you live near where she lives?"

Another little nod. Another wince.

Velda said, "Better lay off with the twenty questions, Mike."

I stood, put my hands on my hips.

"Some gal with yellow hair is missing, and Dekkert wants to know where she went. Judging by the beating he gave Poochie here, Dekkert wants to know bad."

Velda frowned. "Apart from any official police interest, you think?"

"Not necessarily. Typical of these towns to perform their rubber-hose symphonies well away from the station house and out of uniform. That alley makes perfect sense. This town rolls up its sidewalks at sundown, this time of year, with no tourists around."

"Almost no tourists," Velda said.

There was a knock.

"There's the doc now," Velda said.

"Is it?" I asked softly.

I went to the bed where I had tossed my suitcase. I opened it, and slipped the .45 Colt automatic out of its sling where it slept like a baby on my clean underwear. But babies can wake up screaming…

I thumbed off the safety and kicked the slide back and went to the door.

"Yeah?" I said, pointing the snout right where my visitor would be standing.

"It's Moody!" a gruff, age-colored voice called. "This better be important, Mike. I was watching wrestling."

Maybe he'd been down in the bar and I'd missed him.

I raised the snout of the .45, undid the night latch on the door, and opened it. Moody stepped in wearing a wrinkled suit and no tie with his Gladstone bag in hand. He was heavy-set but not fat, white-haired, with a friendly face whose drink-reddened nose held up a pair of wire-rim bifocal glasses.

"So it's our resident beachcomber, is it?" he said idly, giving me a nod to acknowledge my presence. Not much of a greeting, considering after our last evening together I had paid for his night of drinking and hauled his booze-sodden carcass home.

He did more than just nod at Velda. He gave her the kind of smiling, appreciative once-over old men can get away with, taking in a good-looking young gal. He shook his head, sighed, remembering times long past, and gave me a frown that said, *You lucky bastard.*

I clicked the safety on the .45 and shoved it in my waistband.

The doc looked Poochie over for a good ten minutes. He didn't ask him anything that couldn't be answered with a nod or a shake of the head. He approved of Velda's first-aid routine, but had Poochie stand for us to get him out of his ragged clothes and down to his skivvies. The doc went over the cuts and abrasions with alcohol-soaked cotton balls while the little guy squirmed.

Then he gave Poochie a shot and had us walk him over to the bed, where we got him under the covers. Within seconds, the little guy was snoring.

"I don't mind saving his tail," I said to the doc, "but I

am *not* sleeping with that character. Should I get another room?"

"I'll have Percy on the desk send up a rollaway for you, Mike. Somebody needs to be in the room with him tonight."

"How bad is it?"

Moody shrugged. "Surprisingly, not near as bad I would expect. No teeth missing. No indication of internal bleeding. No broken ribs, at least apparently. We'll see if we can get Poochie to come in for some X-rays, tomorrow or the next day. But I will say, it's probably a good thing you came along."

I grunted a laugh. "Dekkert is an old pro at delivering police beatings. He knows just how to mete out punishment and stop short of creating evidence of police brutality."

"A bad apple, all right. He's the deputy chief, but really, he runs things. Chief Beales is local and that helps him get elected. But Beales is soft, a figurehead."

"Corrupt, though?"

"Oh, certainly. You haven't been around in a while, Mike. Things have changed in Sidon."

"Care to fill me in?"

"Maybe later. Over a drink, perhaps."

"Sure, Doc. Listen, is Poochie here slow? You know, simple?"

"You mean retarded? No. But he is on the slow side. I suspect he suffered a trauma, perhaps physical, perhaps mental, when he was young. He's something of an idiot savant."

"Well, is he an idiot or not, Doc?"

He chuckled. "I mean to say, he has an artistic gift that may surprise you. Ask to see his shell collection, while you're around."

That sounded like a blast.

I asked, "You know of any yellow-haired women in town?"

"Why, certainly. We even have a redhead and a brunette or two. And at the moment, we have a particularly lovely black-haired beauty."

He nodded to Velda, gathered his Gladstone bag, and took his leave.

"Nice old boy," Velda said.

"I like him fine. I just wouldn't want to live in a town where his sobriety stood between me and a scalpel."

"That's mean, Mike. Of course, there's nothing worse than a reformed drunk."

"Is that what I am? A reformed drunk?"

"Mike," Velda smiled, her voice low so as not to disturb our slumbering guest, "you're not a reformed anything."

She gathered her overnight bag, and Poochie's dirty, bloody clothes, saying, "I'll wash these." Then she blew me a kiss and was gone.

Almost immediately a knock at the door had me figuring she might have changed her mind. But I took my .45 along, anyway.

It was the rollaway.

The clerk himself brought it—they were clearly short on help before the season started. He seemed to want a tip, but I reminded him about the fin I'd already slipped him.

I had the rollaway unfolded and ready when the phone on the nightstand rang and I got to it before it could disturb Poochie. Not that the sedative the doc gave him would be easily pierced.

"Hammer," I said.

"Mr. Hammer," a mid-range, unctuous voice intoned, "this is Chief of Police Bernard Beales."

Well, whoop de do.

"Chief Beales," I said. "A pleasure."

"Is it, Mr. Hammer?"

"Yeah, and I'm glad you called. Are you aware your deputy chief and two of his pals were beating up a poor little local guy they call Poochie? Right out in public? I had to put a stop to it. Of course, I didn't know they were cops. They were acting more like a goon squad."

"I see. Is that how you're going to play it?"

"It's the truth."

"Do I have to come over to the hotel and have you brought in, Mr. Hammer?"

"No. In fact, I wouldn't advise that. But I'll be glad to come by some time in the morning and straighten this matter out myself."

"You would give yourself up?"

"Why, is there a charge leveled against me?"

"No. Not at this time."

"Fine. Then let's talk about it in the morning. I had kind of a busy evening."

"First thing in the morning, then."

"No, Chiefie. *Some time* in the morning. I'm on vacation. I want to have a nice breakfast and who knows? I might want to take a constitutional along your lovely beach. Surely you want to let me know, as a tourist and the backbone of local economy, that I can come to Sidon and be confident of having a nice getaway."

"Some time tomorrow morning then," he huffed, and hung up.

But I said, "Nighty night, Chiefie," just the same.

Time to beat the sheets. I'd had enough vacation fun for one evening.

CHAPTER TWO

Poochie's shack was a dilapidated affair, rudely constructed from boards drifted in off the tide, that probably never survived a winter without being blown down at least twice. Coming down from a dune, you could see its weathered tin roof displaying faded ads for hot dogs and soft drinks. Trailing after the little guy, Velda and I were pooped by the time we reached his place—we parked the car a good mile away and had to walk the remainder of the distance in ankle-deep sand.

We'd been up around an hour and a half. Back in my hotel room, Poochie had woken with a start and a cry that shook me from a deep sleep and a dream that was a hell of a lot better than sharing a room with a battered beachcomber. But he had settled down quick. He seemed to know that I'd rescued him, and accepted me as his new friend Mike, unquestioningly. I called Velda and she brought around his washed and still a little damp clothes. He grinned at her goofily and just as unquestioningly accepted her as his new friend Velda.

Poochie wolfed down scrambled eggs and bacon and hash browns at a café across the street next to the Sidon Palace, the movie house. Velda and I had the same fare and were damn near as hungry as our guest. I was amazed by his recuperative powers—his face was splotched yellow and purple and his eyes and lips remained puffy, but his manner was happy-go-lucky.

There had been no conversation at breakfast about last night. For Poochie, right now was all there was. He was sitting in a booth with his new pals Mike and Velda, gobbling down good grub, and what had been or would be was irrelevant. Not the worst outlook in the world.

I said we wanted to take him back to his shack, and he said swell, but he needed to pick up some hamburger at the grocery store. We did that, Velda spotting him a buck when Poochie's pockets turned out to be empty. No surprise.

We drove a mile or so till he motioned us to pull over, like a kid who needed a john, and soon we were hiking it in the sand.

In a simple pleated navy skirt and light blue blouse with a sweater slung round her shoulders, my dark-haired secretary looked sexier than any bikini babe this beach had ever seen. Me, I looked like a city slicker in my rumpled suit, even without a tie and with my hat off. But after last night, I needed to go out heeled, and I needed the suitcoat to conceal the .45 in its shoulder sling.

The morning was bright and cool, the ocean breeze refreshing on your face, sun reflecting off shimmering sand, gulls swooping and squawking, the tide lapping, blue ocean glittering, the air salty and fresh, the beach scattered with driftwood and shells, clam, oyster, periwinkle. Good pickings for a beachcomber like Poochie.

Just outside the shack, Velda and I sat down on two old

crates while Poochie ducked inside. In an eye blink the little guy came back out carrying a couple of cats. Scraggly, wild things, they were, but they swarmed all over him in the friendliest way, licking his face and rubbing themselves against his neck. He spread out the pound of hamburger on its butcher paper for them and they dug in together.

When I looked up at Poochie, he was facing the ocean, breathing the salt air, a battered little guy who owned the world. "Ain't it good here, Mike?"

"Swell."

And it was, as far as it went. But what he called home was a barrel to hold fish heads, three crude fishing poles set against the side of the shack, an ancient wheelbarrow to gather shells, two cats for company, and a broken-down shanty to keep the rain off his head.

"Come on inside," he said brightly. "I got lots of things I want to show you."

We followed him in, ducking our heads as we went. He put a match to an oil lamp and the pale orange light threw flickering shadows on the wall. A homemade table sat in the middle, around which were four more crates for chairs. Why he bothered with four, I don't know. I doubt if he ever had company. A single bunk was built against the far wall, covered with somebody's cast-off quilt. Behind the table a stove of iron pipes was overlaid on some bricks with a firewood bin next to it. For utensils there were two pots, some reclaimed and polished cans, several old knives and forks, and a wooden salad spoon.

What interested me most was the half-carved shell on the makeshift table. Beside it was a well-worn shoemaker's leather knife. I picked up the shell and ran my hands over the picture carved there. It was beautiful—a manger scene with an angel in the background. The dog-eared Christmas card it was copied from lay under the knife.

He was grinning. Where his teeth weren't yellow, they were black. "Like it, Mike?"

"You said it," I grinned at him. "Where did you learn to do this?"

"In school." He said it proudly.

"No kidding?" I couldn't believe he'd stayed in school long enough to develop this kind of skill. The detail work was fantastic.

"Yup. That's where I went when I was little. I remember it real good. I can hardly remember anything else about being a kid except the school. They were good to me there and a priest showed me how to carve wood. I did bad in all my studies, Mike, but not carving. That priest said I had a real talent. Then he got me a shell one day and I carved that. I got plenty of 'em. Look!"

He pointed to the walls and I whistled under my breath. They were arrayed on a two-by-four running around three walls, beautiful examples of what a simple mind could do if it concentrated.

He pointed to some beat-up cabinets below the crude shelving; they probably had been scavenged from the galley of some old boat. "I got lots more. Down here is my private collection."

Velda whispered to me: "Idiot savant."

Why did everybody keep saying that! I *knew* this guy was an idiot.

But like Doc Moody said, an idiot with a touch of genius. Each shell was a masterpiece of craftsmanship. Some were carved into animals, others were seascapes, all worked into the rounded exterior of a shell. The pale light of the lantern hardly brought out the exquisite pink and cream tones. I knew people in the city who would pay top dollar for these.

I asked, "Ever sell any, Poochie?"

"Sure, I sell 'em. The stuff I keep on that one shelf, those are for sale." He pointed. "That's how I get all my money."

His little shack wasn't exactly a showroom. "How much do you get, Poochie? And who buys them?"

"Oh, a nice man from the city comes by and gives me a whole dollar a piece for 'em. That's pretty darn good, ain't it, Mike?"

"That's good, all right, but don't you sell any more until I see the guy that buys them."

"Why… sure, Mike. He'll be here in a few days."

"Great. Let me act as your agent. All great artists need agents."

"You think I'm a great artist, Mike?"

"I sure do. How often does he come around, this guy?"

"Always around this time every month he comes."

I would kick the crap out of the bastard for taking advantage of Poochie like that. A buck a piece and he was probably raking in a hundred per, anyway.

"I'll negotiate a new price."

Velda was walking around the little room, looking at the individual shells on the shelf, breathless at the sheer beauty of them.

I got up and put a hand on her shoulder. "I want to take a walk up the beach. Care to come?"

She shook her head, the dark tresses bouncing. "No. You go ahead. I've had my fill of walking on sand for a while. I'll just stick around here and enjoy the view."

Soon we were back on the beach where she had kicked off her sandals and was lifting her skirt to wade in the tide, her gaze on the expanse of blue that a world away joined the other expanse of blue above. The wind was making lovely dark streaming tendrils of her long raven hair, as if she were underwater. Who needed mermaids?

I started off with Poochie at my heels.

When we were out of earshot of Velda, I said, "Show me where that lady lives—the one with the yellow hair."

As we rounded a dune, he pointed between a number of trees that stood in a row, like a tall fence designed to keep one half of the beach away from the other.

"Right up there, Mike. That's where she lives. You're not gonna go up there, are you?" He seemed fearful.

"No, Poochie, not now."

I took in the place from a better angle. It was a magnificent home, built like an old colonial mansion right down to the twenty-foot pillars surrounding the entire structure. Set back a few hundred yards from the ocean, it commanded a superb view from the top of a slight rise. Earth must have been shipped in to make a terrace on either side, as its color was the bright green of lawn grass and not the duller shade of the sand variety.

From the rear of the house that faced the water, a flagstone path curved down to the trees and ended abruptly at a gazebo whose latticework was covered with ivy.

A little warning sign was tacked to the tree nearest the sandy beach. Poochie stayed behind, nervous, as I walked up for a better look. It read:

PRIVATE PROPERTY
KEEP OFF!
E.J. WESLEY

I grinned. Now I knew who the lady with the yellow hair was.

Sharron Wesley.

You probably read about her yourself—the infamous, two-timing ex-chorus tomato that stood charges for murdering her millionaire husband and got off scot-free when an all-male jury paid more attention to her legs than the testimony.

I remembered that case well, though I knew it strictly from the spectator seats. Because of Sharron, two husbands had died. Even before she married Wesley, she had spent a term in the big house for manslaughter of hubby number one: a glorified pimp of a manager that she claimed beat her. Well, he hadn't been beating her when she smothered him in his sleep. But the tabloids had loved that yellow hair and those long chorus-girl gams that she wasn't shy about showing off only to jurors— reporters got in on the fun, as well.

Still, what the hell her second husband ever saw in her was more than I could see. There are plenty of good-looking fluffs around Manhattan that don't smother their hubbies in bed. Of course, Wesley had died due to his bad heart, right? That digitalis overdose was just an accident on curvy Sharron's part.

And ever since, she had been using his dough to support a revolving door of gigolos and a gambling habit and a general party-girl good time. I knew her a little, and she had tried to make me more than once, but I'd sooner sleep with a snake. Last time I saw her, at the Zero Zero Club, she was crocked to the gills.

According to Pat, the D.A. had plenty to hang her with, but the shyster she had pleading her case did a fine job of screwing up the facts. The scandal sheets went crazy over the angle shots of her legs and the jury was drooling half the time. The judge who sat on the case almost blew his top at the verdict, telling that jury he'd never seen a greater miscarriage of justice in his courtroom, shooing them out in disgust.

If these fancy beach-side digs were any indication, Mrs. Wesley must have inherited her husband's money intact and decided on this modest playpen instead of her penthouse on Central Park to establish a residence.

Only now she was gone.

A missing person.

And last night Dekkert had damn near crippled a nice simple-minded joe just to squeeze out any morsel of information about her whereabouts. No doubt Dekkert figured that the Wesley dame would have been seen, if she had taken off through town. Her car would be well known in this vicinity. Otherwise, beachcomber Poochie was in a fine spot to see anything and everything that went on at the mansion, even if he didn't pay particular attention to it.

But why was Dekkert interested?

Sharron had a perfect right to go where she pleased. So what if she took off by boat, or with some out-of-towner in a strange car that wouldn't raise any notice rolling through sleepy Sidon? She'd been gone a week. And a week wasn't so long as to warrant an investigation when there were no suspicious circumstances.

Or were there?

The only thing I was sure of was that something foul was in the ocean breeze and I was going to find out what. I had tangled with Dekkert before and was not about to let him get away with making a punching bag out of an innocent schnook like Poochie.

Velda had fallen asleep on the sand when I got back. She had spread out that light sweater and was nestled down on it, her sweet, sultry face turned to one side. I gave her gentle prods with my toe until she looked up at me sleepily.

"Time to get up already?" she purred, stretching her arms.

"Rise and shine," I said. "We have to go."

"Where?"

"Town. I have a date."

"Do tell!"

"With the police chief."

She got to her feet in an instant. Her eyes narrowed, and the pretty mouth got as ugly as it could, which wasn't very ugly.

"I get it, you louse. You're going to work. I can see myself already, chasing all over Sidon doing your legwork. Well, if you think—"

"Aw, kitten, take it easy. I only—"

"You 'only' nothing. When you get that look on your face, it means trouble. We came up here for a vacation. You're here for *a* rest, not to make *an* arrest."

"You're imagining things."

"If we are not here for rest and relaxation, big boy, I am going home."

She turned and started to walk away, but I put out my hand and stopped her, turned her to me. She had tears in her eyes.

"Mike, don't ruin this…"

"Hey, kid, I'm not drinkin', am I? I'm just curious about what's going on out here in the sticks."

"Leave the curiosity to those scraggly cats, why don't you?"

Poochie edged up near us and said, "Golly, Mike, why do you make the nice lady cry when you like her so much? I can tell you do."

When he realized what he had said, he turned his head and blushed. It was so silly and cute that both Velda and I wound up grinning at each other.

Then her expression turned serious and her dark eyes took on a sensual cast. "*Do* you, Mike?"

"What?"

"*Like* me… *so much*?"

I looked at her. She was as pretty as anything I had ever seen. Tall, jet black hair, always in that sweeping pageboy that I so admired. Big and beautiful with more curves than a mountain road…

She was warm under my hands. I tilted her chin and bent my head. Her mouth found mine and she trembled under me as our mouths surrendered to each other.

When I held her away from me, she was gasping. "That was the first time you ever did that, Mike."

"I've wanted to for a long time," I told her roughly.

"Why?" Her eyes were soft and inviting. I ran my fingers through her hair.

"You know why. A dame works for a guy, and it gets out of hand, and all of a sudden—"

"Shut-up and kiss me again."

I did, but then Poochie was right there watching us with a big smile plastered on his baby-face mug. The kiss turned into a mutual laugh, and then I tugged at her arm.

"Let's go, Velda."

She just nodded.

We were already walking when I called back, "So long, Poochie!"

"So long! You'll come see me *again*, won't you?"

"Sure will!" we said together.

As we glanced back, we saw him dash into the shanty and come out with a shell. He rushed to us and handed it to Velda.

"A pretty present for the pretty lady," he said with a shy grin.

Velda took it, looking pleased. It was his latest, the Nativity scene.

"Why, thank you, Poochie," she said. "It's beautiful."

When we were walking back to the car, she squeezed my arm and lay her head against my shoulder. "I like

Poochie, too, Mike. Maybe we shouldn't leave Sidon until we know he's safe."

"Yeah." I lit up a Lucky. "I have to make sure that Dekkert character isn't a threat to him."

"You're a softie, underneath it all, aren't you?"

"Yeah. All squishy."

"If it weren't for Poochie back there, I'd still be thinking you were just an old so-and-so."

I blew a cloud of cigarette smoke and broke out my lopsided smile.

"Kitten," I said, pretending to be shocked. "Watch your language."

They were waiting for me when I ambled into the police station. I hoped they'd enjoyed themselves, speculating on what they'd do to me.

There was a counter at right, but otherwise this was a fair-sized bullpen of half a dozen desks. Everybody from last night was there—the athlete, the scarecrow and Dekkert, of course. But today they were in police uniforms. Somebody reached for a phone while I stood there jamming a butt in my sneer and firing it up.

Then a fat slob in a too-small uniform and a too-large cap squeezed out through a wood-and-pebbled glass door that said CHIEF OF POLICE. His face was a bloated red mask of fury; all the purple veins in his nose had dilated until it looked like a cross section of a Martian landscape. His thick lips were working with anger at the thought of anyone flaunting his authority.

"Morning, Chiefie," I said with a respectful nod.

Chief Beales said nothing. Just froze between his office and me.

Dekkert was sitting behind one of the front two desks

with veins popping on his forehead and cords standing out on his neck, but most of his face was hidden behind a swathing of bandages. If he wore an expression I couldn't see it. Not that I gave a damn.

He pulled his bulk from the chair and got to his feet, fists clenched into a pair of hams. The cops on either side of him tried to keep him back behind that desk, with hands on his shoulders.

"Let him go," I said, with a dismissive wave.

They did.

He came out and around the desk, moving at me as though he were going to beat my brains out. Maybe he thought last night was a fluke. If he did, he changed his mind in a hurry.

I never moved.

He stopped in front of me, breathing heavily in my face. No onions this time. Tabasco on his morning eggs, maybe.

The big man seemed almost insane with anger. "I ought to *kill* you, Hammer!"

"Dekkert, I told you a long time ago, back in the city," I said casually, "you are welcome to try it. Any time."

Every word I spoke must have gone through him like a knife. He just stood there, his huge chest rising and falling to where his badge might pop off. I could see him trying to force himself to make a move.

I laughed in his face. "You're not going to try anything, Dekkert."

His teeth were clenched and his eyes showed white all round. "I'm *not*? And why is *that*, Hammer?"

"Because you're yellow."

I put my mitt in his puss and shoved. As he stumbled back against his desk, everybody in the room stopped breathing. Except me.

The bastard's eyes made narrow slits.

I grinned at him.

His hand streaked for the gun at his hip. I let him get it out before I bothered to move. But when I did, it was faster than his eyes could follow. I fired from a crouch and his gun spun out of his hand and clunked to the floor, while from the corner of my eye I saw wood chips fly from the desk, barely a foot away from the chief.

Dekkert was looking at his gun hand, and the ragged red groove carved there, amazed.

I got to my feet, the .45 still in hand, waiting to see if any of these other fine officers of the law had anything to say or do about what just happened.

They didn't. They were too busy standing there shaking like somebody opened a door and let in a cold damn wind.

Finally I shoved my gun back under my shoulder, sauntered over to Dekkert and grabbed a handful of his shirt. With the back of my free hand, I smashed him across the bridge of that nebulous nose. He tried to pull away, but he wasn't *that* big. I hit him twice again, until blood stained the bandages on his face.

"You forgot something, Dekkert," I informed him, his shirt in my fist holding him up, depriving his feet of the floor. "You forgot that I practice with my rod and can get it out in a fraction of a second. And you forgot something else. I never take it out unless I intend to use it. The next time you pull a on gun me, I put one between your eyes."

I turned to the rest of them, moving from one face to another. "That goes for the rest of you goof-offs. Spread the word to any off-duty brothers in blue."

I pushed Dekkert away. He was holding his gauze-covered face, peering at me from between his fingers, like a child afraid Daddy would get out the razor strop next.

Somewhere along the way I'd lost my smoke. I got out

my Luckies, jammed a fresh one in, let the Zippo set fire to the tip, and turned casually toward the fat florid chief. "Now, what was it you wanted to see me about, Chiefie? You said to stop in."

The chief tugged at his coat and backed away, looking toward the athlete and scarecrow for assistance, but they didn't know quite what to do. Cops, they called themselves. Cops hell. I wished Pat Chambers of the New York Homicide Bureau had been here to see this travesty.

Somehow Beales managed to clear his throat. He pointed toward whence he'd come. "In my office, Mr. Hammer."

"No, Chiefie. Right here is fine."

He was trembling, too.

"Oh, for Pete's sake, relax. I'm not going to bite you."

The fatso finally backed himself up against the desk where Dekkert had been sitting. Sidon's police chief was sweating profusely. I walked over next to him and parked on the desktop, picking splinters from the spot where my bullet clipped it.

"Now you look here," he spluttered, "this is a police station. You can't waltz in here and intimidate my men! Pulling a gun and firing it *here*—are you insane, man?"

I didn't bother pointing out that Dekkert had gone for his gun first.

"That's pretty much what I told Dekkert last night," I remarked dryly. "Not to bother trying to intimidate me. Let's hear something new."

There was silence for a few seconds, then, "I could have you arrested."

"Go ahead," I invited, "and see what happens. My one phone call won't be to my attorney, though. I'll ring up the State's Attorney's office. They don't have to be told that you and your punks aren't cops, just political appointees. They know all about these small towns. Like I do."

The chief decided he'd carry on his questioning from a chair between his two men, and got behind Dekkert's desk to do so. He pulled a cigar from his pocket and bit the end off nervously. The scarecrow provided a flame. The chief got the stogie going, his eyes moving with thought as he searched for a way to handle me.

Right then I figured I'd let them know just where I stood. I spoke between drags on the Lucky.

"Let's get something straight, ladies. I came here for a vacation, that's all. I wasn't on any case, I knew nothing about the fun and games going on in Sidon lately… until now. But for your information I'm going to cut myself a slice of this cake. I don't know what's really shaking around here, but if Dekkert has his nose in it, it must be dirty."

Dekkert, who was plopped in a rear chair, as far away from me as he could get, said nothing.

"I wasn't born yesterday," I reminded them, "so stay out of my way. You try any funny business and I'll have a slew of reporters from the city down here and they'll tear this town wide open. Or if you really get tough, you'll find some connections of mine ripping into you with everyone from the governor on down behind them. Follow?"

Chief Beales swallowed. And nodded.

"Good. Now that we have that straight, let's get down to cases. Why did you want to see me?"

Beales made an indignant sniff. "You know why, Mr. Hammer—what is your interest in a certain local woman's disappearance?"

"I told you on the phone last night. These overgrown members of the Hitler youth here were playing kick the can with your local beachcomber filling in as the can."

"And you broke it up. Fine. But why did you take that dimwit back to your hotel room last night?"

I hopped from the desk ready to smack his teeth down

his throat, but the two cops were covering him, hands on the butts of guns at their sides. I leaned my nose in till it was almost touching the chief's.

"You louse," I told him. "What did you want me to do, let him lie there and bleed? Suppose I came along and you were in trouble, and did the same thing to you? Not that it wouldn't be a pleasure."

I backed away a little.

He licked his lips again. "That's not the point, Mr. Hammer."

"The hell it's not. When you couldn't get what you wanted out of Poochie, you gave him the iron boot. Why? Just to warn him to keep his mouth shut? What a community. Either the citizens here are blind or just plain stupid. If Poochie had enough sense, he'd hire a lawyer and drag your sorry tails into court so fast it would make your heads swim."

"Look, Hammer—"

"Not *Mister* Hammer anymore? Don't worry, chum, that score isn't settled yet. I'm going to cover that little guy if no one else will. Anything happens to him, I'll give each of you sons of bitches the kind of questioning that you gave Poochie… only worse. Dekkert already got his, Chiefie… push me, and you'll get yours for letting it happen."

Dekkert let out a low rumble from the back of the room. The bandages were more red than white now, good and soaked, but the bleeding from his smashed nose had stopped. Whether that rumble was a nonverbal comment or just some pain finding its way out, I couldn't say.

But Dekkert was one guy I was going to have to keep an eye on. He'd be out to get me, and he wouldn't come at me fair next time; but he wasn't going to get the chance. Not if I could help it.

Right now, however, he wasn't in the mood to talk

much, unless he wanted to gag on his own gore.

Beales came back with: "What did that addle-brained beachcomber *tell* you?"

"What he told you. Nothing. Sharron Wesley is missing and you think he either saw something or had something to do with it."

The chief goggled at me. "How do you know her name?"

"I get around. My God, it's so damn evident the Wesley dame's your missing yellow-haired gal, you couldn't hide it under a mountain. Now let me ask you something. What was she doing around here that makes her disappearance so extraordinary?"

The chief lifted his little chin and several more chins came along for the ride. "I'll have you know she's a permanent resident of Sidon. A most respected citizen. And we look after all our citizens."

"Like Poochie?" My laugh was drenched in sarcasm. "Or is the special treatment reserved for the citizens that have the money to pay you off, and keep 'em covered?"

It was a shot in the dark—that the rich missing dame had the local cops working security for her—but it hit home. If something happened to her on their watch, their meal ticket would be gone, or they might be in Dutch.

The red drained from the chief's face and his mouth opened, but nothing came out. The two cops looked at him quickly, then at Dekkert, who gave a nervous twitch from his corner.

The chief's eyes disappeared into slits in the fat puss. Finally he asked, "What do you mean by that, Hammer?"

I'd be damned if I was going to let them know I was taking potshots in the dark.

"What the hell do you think?" I said.

I shoved my hat on the back of my head and yawned.

"Well, boys and girls," I said, "if you don't have anything else for me on this fine morning, I'll just be running along. You know where to find me."

The chief swallowed again. "How long will you be in Sidon, Mr. Hammer?"

Mister Hammer again.

I'd been meaning to go back Sunday night, but I said, "Oh, I'll be around for another week or so. Maybe I can help you out some. Take it easy."

At the door I stopped and added, "One other thing. Tell that zombie of a night clerk at the Sidon Arms something for me, would you?"

"Uh… what is that, Mr. Hammer?"

"That I'll stuff that hotel register up his ass if he does any more spying on me."

I shut the door quietly. No need to slam it, and be rude.

CHAPTER THREE

Back at the hotel, I found Velda in a booth in the bar, busily sopping up a highball and working a crossword puzzle at the same time.

"Little early for that, isn't it?" I asked, nodding to the highball.

"I'm on vacation," she said.

I slid in opposite her. "Interesting way to keep Mike on the wagon—start drinking early."

She gave me her cutest smile and took a lady-like sip. "I don't want you on the wagon. I just want you sober."

I grinned at her, said, "I like the way you think," and called for a beer.

Usually by this time she'd be in a bathing suit, but for once she had on clothes. The day was a little too cool for sunning and swimming, I guessed. She shoved the paper away and leaned toward me, big brown eyes wide, long lashes fluttering like lazy butterflies.

"So, Mike—what did you find out?"

"What makes you think I found anything out? The police chief wanted to see me."

"Right. What did you find out?"

The bartender, a lanky guy wrapped in an apron and boredom, delivered my nice cold mug of beer. I waited until he moved away before I told Velda about the little set-to at police headquarters. She made a great audience, moving from surprise to fear to laughter at all the right times.

When I'd wrapped it up, she said, "What do you think, Mike? What goes on in this town? And what does the Wesley woman have to do with it?"

"I don't know yet."

"You know what your next move is?"

I wiped suds off my mouth with the back of a hand. "Get out to the Wesley house and take a look around. Sharron wasn't the type to live quietly. Whatever she was up to has the boys in blue here worried plenty."

"What about them? Are they the power in Sidon?"

"Don't be silly. If there's anything big going on, it takes more brains than they have collectively to run it. Those guys are stooges, especially the chief. Dekkert is a plain out-and-out strong-arm boy. When the report reaches the top man that there's an outsider prying around, that's when the fun will begin. You just watch."

"Watch my eye," Velda countered. "I'm tired of sitting still while things go round and round. How about letting me in on something for a change? Don't forget I have a private op's license and a permit to carry a gun. I won't get hurt."

Some girl, Velda. Next to her compact in her purse nestled a flat .32 automatic and she knew how to use it. And that wasn't her only weapon—she could whip off a heel and crack a masher's skull in a flash.

I patted her hand. "You don't get the point, honey. If this was an ordinary routine job, I'd say swell, but it's not. It's a damn dirty business and I'd hate like hell to see you in over your head."

"Mike… I'm a big girl."

"And in all the right places. Look, if you really want to help me, just do as I tell you. Maybe what I ask you might seem insignificant, but I promise it won't be. I can't be in two places at the same time, and the little details you take care of help out a lot."

"Okay, Mike," Velda said softly, through a pouty smile. "You're the boss."

We finished our drinks and ordered another round. I tried to think through what I had so far, but there was really nothing to go on except a disappearance and something that smelt like power politics and graft. I needed more.

"Wait here for a minute," I said to Velda.

She shrugged and went back to her crossword.

I went over to the bartender and got change for a five spot, mostly quarters, and went to a pay phone booth in the back of the room. I stuck a nickel in and asked for the operator.

When I got her, I said, "Police Headquarters in New York City," then rattled off the number.

The switchboard at HQ knew to put me right through to the man I'd called.

"Captain Chambers, Homicide Bureau, speaking."

"Hello, kid. This is Mike. Sober and sassy."

"Well, about time you gave me a buzz. How goes the getaway?"

"About as well as that time Dillinger and Baby Face Nelson went to that lodge in Wisconsin."

He laughed, but said, "I hope you're kidding. How's Sidon look to you?"

"Dead on its feet, but right now the only tourists in town are Velda and me. It'll get livelier."

"You mean when the season opens? Or because *you're* in town? I can tell that this is no social call. What's up?"

"Not very much… yet. Do you have any information on Sharron Wesley dating from after the trial? I mean, has she been booked for anything or been connected with anything shady?"

"So why the sudden interest in Sharron Wesley?"

That guy had a hair-trigger mind that could figure angles faster than I could snap my fingers. I was willing to bet that he had already mentally reviewed the Wesley dame's entire past including the most recent episodes involving the tabloids' favorite black widow.

"She seems to be Sidon's most prominent notorious citizen," I said. "Humor me."

"Just a minute," he said, "let me check my files."

He was back in seconds and I could hear the rustle of paper as he thumbed through. "Yeah, here's something. Mrs. Wesley was given a ticket for illegal parking on an express street about a month ago."

"That it?"

"No. No… then she was arrested for disturbing the peace two days later."

"Interesting."

"There's more. She had a catfight with another babe in a night club. Seems like it continued out onto the street after they were put out of the place and a window got broken. She paid for the window and her fine."

"She can afford to."

"The last time she was in the custody of the city was two weeks ago. Mrs. Wesley was picked up when the vice squad raided a high-stakes card game in a suite of rooms in a downtown hotel. She was released along with three other women who apparently weren't in on the game."

"Pat, you're not saying this was prostitution. She's not a damn call girl."

"I don't know what she is, other than not a grieving widow. We've had some big-time gamblers in town lately, Mike, and she might have been backing somebody's play. She can afford that, too."

"Yes, she can."

"Anyway, pal, that's all I have." I heard the file hit his desk like a slap. "Okay, I showed you mine, now you show me yours—what gives on your end?"

I started from the beginning and took it through to the police station visit this morning.

When I finished, he muttered, "Dekkert, huh?"

"Yup."

"Would it surprise you to hear I've had all kinds of bad reports on that bastard since he was kicked off the force?"

"Nope."

"Seems Dekkert got in a jam in Miami, working for a security outfit that was burgling its own clients. Somehow he managed not to do any time—maybe he ratted his gang out. Then he wasn't heard from until we got a teletype from San Francisco requesting his history. He landed a private dick's license there, and during the course of a case beat a guy to death. When they caught up with him, his license got revoked and he was given twenty-four hours to get out of the state."

"Sounds like he manages to leave dirty smudges on his record when it should be filthy as hell."

Pat grunted agreement. "Dekkert's always had a way of finding some mob angel to cover for him. When the trouble hits, he makes a deal, pays off whoever he has to, and starts somewhere else."

"But how can he wrangle another police job, even in Sidon?"

"Mike, he was asked to resign from the New York force. The administration at that time had too much dirty laundry to risk exposing every lousy racket Dekkert was tied into. Read his jacket and you'll see medals of valor, between those dirty smudges. This is one very hard case. Be careful of him, chum."

"Don't worry about me," I laughed. "After the two beatings I gave him, he knows what to expect now."

"Yeah, but do you?"

"Pat, I'm just in Sidon to take the rest cure, remember? Anyway, thanks for the info. If something develops, I'll ring you."

"Always glad to help you out. It's the least I can do, all the times you come through for me. But the truth is, Mike… I ought to forget I even know you, after the Williams case*."

"Pat, I took this trip to forget about all that, remember?"

"I remember. Do you?"

"Pat…"

"You run into a crooked cop you tangled with before, and stumble into a missing persons case, which incidentally hasn't come over the teletype as such yet. And you tell a very amusing story about shooting up the Sidon police station."

"I didn't shoot it up. I just—"

"Shot a gun out of the deputy chief's hand. What's your horse in this race, Mike? You got no murdered friend to avenge this time."

"Back off, Pat."

* The Williams Case, from *I, the Jury*

"Okay, I will. And I will help you like I always do. Whatever background info you need, buddy, you got it. You just have to convince me of one thing."

"What's that?"

"That you aren't down at Sidon trying to get yourself killed."

"Pat," I said. "I don't have *that* big a conscience."

After I hung up, the operator came on wanting another quarter to cover the call, and I fed it to her.

I returned to Velda's booth and she looked up and asked, "Now what?"

"That was Pat. He couldn't give me any help except to provide a little something on Sharron Wesley."

"A little something good?"

I shook my head. "She was nabbed on a few minor violations. Dekkert must have picked this podunk as a last resort or else he's working for something or somebody bigger than the so-called police department."

"Why last resort?"

"He's been in a few nasty jams since he was run out of Manhattan. Want another drink?"

"No thanks, Mike."

"Maybe some lunch?"

"I'm still stuffed from breakfast. There's a theater down the street with a Saturday matinee double feature." She scooted out of the booth. "What do you say?"

For the next two and a half hours we sat through a western we'd already seen and a Bowery Boys comedy I wished we never had. I wasn't really paying any attention to the screen, just sitting there going over everything I'd learned so far, again and again. Finally I fell asleep and Velda punched me in the ribs when it was time to leave.

As we exited, Velda said, "You looked surprised when I woke you."

"Yeah. I was wondering what Huntz Hall was doing in a Randolph Scott picture."

We headed across the street to a dingy diner, boxcar-style; but the kitchen behind the counter looked clean and the cutlery didn't have food caked in the tines of the forks like a lot of such joints. The proprietor was a big jovial Polack who sported a handlebar mustache and a pair of black eyebrows that met in the middle without thinning out in the slightest.

He wiped the counter clean enough for eating, then said, "What'll it be, folks?"

"I'll have the veal cutlet," Velda said. "Home fries and corn."

I asked, "Got a steak?"

He shook his head and black snakes danced on his scalp. "Naw. Rationing is over, my friend, but there are still shortages."

"I know. Just asking."

"Oh, I could have plenty of meat if I wanted to buy black market, but I won't do it. I lost a son on Iwo and I'll be damned if I will do business with them sons of…" He hesitated. "…excuse me, miss… dirty bums who made all that filthy dough while our kids were dying over there."

"Gimme the cutlet then."

"Okay. You don't like my speech?"

"Your speech was swell. But it's not what I came in for. Veal cutlet."

He looked at me carefully, trying to decide whether we were friends or not. "You in the war, mister?"

"He sure was," Velda piped up.

I growled, "Velda…"

"With the infantry in the Pacific," she went on. "He killed more Japs than the Enola Gay."

A grin bloomed and took the handlebar along for

the ride. "No kidding? I was down in Port Moresby, cooking... till they kicked me out."

I asked, "How come?"

Our plates of food were already in the window behind him.

He went to get them, and said to us over his shoulder, "They found out I was over-age. Ain't that something? Gee, I worked harder than any two kids in the outfit. Over-age, huh, what a joke. What a bad joke on me."

"How did they get wise?"

He set the plates in front of us; their steam smelled good. "The pencil pushers did it, but it took a while. See, I was in the first war, only I wasn't a cook, I was in the tanks. Took 'em a year and a half to catch up, but they did. When I left, the colonel, he shook my hand. Don'tcha think that was nice of him?"

I laughed. The Polack was a good egg. I had met up with his kind before—strictly square shooters. As I dug into the meal, I could see why he did a fairly good business during the day. The cutlets were done to a turn, and there was no skimping on the vegetables. Finally a good guy to know in Sidon.

Between mouthfuls, I asked, "Say, who's this Wesley woman out on the shore?"

"That whoor..." He looked at Velda again, though she was too busy eating to pay any attention, and not nearly as easily offended as he imagined. "...that *trollop*," he continued. "Lots of wild parties, brings her drunken friends to town and they wreck the place. Always a crowd from the city, they are."

"Can't the police take care of that?"

"Are you kidding, mister? The cops here, they got the hand out for all they can get and, brother, does Mrs. Wesley play ball with them. One of the guys that was out to her house killed a kid when he was driving his car drunk and he never did a day behind bars. She gave the kid's folks ten thousand smackers and they had to shut up."

Velda and I exchanged a troubled glance.

I asked him, "Why don't the taxpayers object? They appoint the cops around here, don't they?"

"Sure they do. Like they appoint the mayor. Everyone does just what Rudy Holden wants them to do, or else they find some other town to live in."

"Rudy who?"

"Holden. Rudolph Holden, Rudy. Hell, mister, he waves the flag around Sidon. The winter people only live here so they can operate during the summer. They own beach houses or have concessions along the street for the visitors. If they don't play ball with Rudy, they don't get no license. That's all there is to it."

"How about you?"

He grinned again, white teeth flashing through the dark mustache. "Oh, Rudy and his boys, they don't fool around with me."

"You're an exception, huh? How did you pull that off?"

He pounded his chest with a fist. "I come from a big family, mister. I got twelve brothers and four sons left. When the boys in the blue uniforms come around for the summer shakedown, I tell them that maybe I might have a family reunion soon. They know what I mean." The guy laughed from the bottom of his barrel chest. "And I'm the smallest one in the family. My brothers are pretty big. They raise plenty hell around this place when they get started."

I grinned at him. "I hear this Dekkert is a pretty tough apple himself."

"Maybe not no more," he said, pulling on his mustache, thoughtful and still grinning. "Word around town is, some big guy whopped the devil out of him."

"You don't say," I said.

Velda had a pixie grin going. She caught the Pollack's eyes and pointed her fork at me.

"Hey!" he blurted. "Are *you* the guy? Tony said it was some big ugly guy from out of town! Are you him?"

I laughed. "I fit the description."

"I don't mean no disrespect." He stuck out a big hand. "Lemme shake with you."

We did. His grip didn't break my fingers, but stopped just short.

"By damn, it's good to see *somebody* in this town what ain't scared of them stinking cops! The meal's on the house. You and your girl both. Wait'll I tell little Steve about you! What's your *name*, mister?"

"Mike Hammer. I'm a private dick from New York."

"Good one, too," Velda said, pointing the fork again. "Pretty famous."

"Hammer." His eyes popped. "*Mike Hammer*! Well, I'll be a dirty name. I *got* it now. *I* read the *Daily News*! Ain't you the one that—"

Velda stopped him again. "Shot down those two hoods in Times Square? That's him. Showed a couple hundred people in a nightclub what a crook had for dinner, using a steak knife? One and the same. Got in Dutch with the police for making a perfectly good suspect unrecognizable? That's him."

"Cut it out, chick." I nudged her in the ribs. "I'm not so bad."

"Oh, no," she said, very sarcastically. "He's good with the 'chicks,' too."

She just had to tack that on. She always does.

The big man slapped his chest. "Well, me, I'm Steve Kowalski. Just call me Big Steve. Is the pretty lady your wife?"

"Not yet. This is Velda, my secretary and good right arm."

"She is very beautiful," he said, "your right arm."

Velda gave him a warm smile, and then me one—she liked the sound of that "not yet." I better watch my step or she'd be pinning me down with a proposal and I wasn't near ready.

Over a piece of pie and a second cup of coffee, Big Steve told us what he knew about the town. The winter population was about fifteen hundred, but it increased to ten thousand during the summer months, most of the crowd attracted from New York. The beach was nice, and there were few limitations on parties, drinking bouts in saloons, or what have you. From his description, Sidon was the Reno of Long Island.

I asked, "There's illegal gambling here, Steve?"

"There is." He held up his hands as if in surrender. "But I don't know where and don't want to. I keep apart from that."

But he knew in general what was going on. He knew Sidon was situated far enough away from everything for visitors to enjoy loosely enforced laws, and yet not far enough away to hamper travel. Dotted along the shore line were the mansions of the wealthy. Some lived here all year round, but most boarded up their fancy pads for use during the summertime only.

These people had nothing to do with the town. Even the bulk of their provisions came in from the outside, and their recreation was on their own private beaches.

Velda said, "Anything for a young couple like us to do after dark, before the season starts around here?"

I could think of something.

Big Steve said, "There's a nice beer parlor just down the street—jukebox and everything. But you don't wanna eat there."

"Okay," she said. "What else?"

"There's a place on the highway where you kids can do some serious drinkin' and dancin'. Only opened up a few days ago—gettin' the jump on the season. They got a little band. Not bad."

"Sounds good," Velda said. Then to me she said, "Let's try it, after work."

Big Steve, who was down from us now using the rag on the counter, said, "Work? You two are *working*?"

"It's not my idea," Velda smirked.

"Zip it," I told her.

A screaming siren grabbed our attention and we spun on our stools to see a Sidon police car shoot by. Simultaneously a little barefooted kid ran into the diner, his hair flying in excitement.

"*Uncle Steve!* They found a dead lady in the park! She's sitting on the stone horse... and she ain't got no *clothes* on!"

That was all I needed to hear.

With Velda inches behind me, I ran out and toward the hotel to get the heap out of the lot. Soon I was behind the wheel and swinging around in the middle of the street and racing through town, following the banshee wail.

The park was a mile and a half outside town, a fifty-acre grove of trees and lawn built on reclaimed land to provide the town's only public bathing beach. On the shore were the dressing houses, with closed buildings that became soda and hot dog concessions during the summer. In the midst of the tree-rimmed park itself, twin paths curved in from one end of the beach to the other, circling around the granite figure of a horse set directly on the ground, supposedly drinking from an artificial spring, now dry.

I ran the car into the parking lot behind a dozen others. Evidently news traveled fast in this little town and, considering Sidon's size, there were a lot of curiosity seekers.

Velda and I wasted no time. We took the right-hand path and half-ran toward the horse. Clouds were protecting the sun from the unpleasantness and keeping the park cool and blue. Ahead of us a loud voice through a hand-speaker was ordering people to keep back and keep moving. Seemed the Sidon PD had at least six officers, because they were spread out keeping people away from the grim discovery. The crowd was a mix of ages and were clearly not tourists. Some kids were mixed in, too, getting some Saturday afternoon education.

With Velda tagging after, I broke through the crowd and the skinny cop I'd elbowed in the nuts the night before blocked me, putting out his hand in "stop" fashion. I gave him one look and he dropped his hand reluctantly, and stepped aside.

There on the well-trimmed grass a dozen feet from the base of the statue was Dekkert, crisply uniformed, his face criss-crossed with a fresh set of bandages. With him was Chief Beales. Both were speaking to a nondescript, pot-bellied little guy in a short-sleeve white shirt with a too-short necktie. I caught the name Holden once, and realized I was looking at the town boss. He certainly didn't look like anything more than the manager of a grocery store.

All three men stopped talking at one point, and shot sideways glances our way as we neared, but that was all. I could see them later.

Right now I wanted a closer look at that horse and the naked rider it bore.

She was there all right. Not sitting as the kid had

described, but draped over the back of the statue. She was face down, her bright yellow hair hanging limply between her dangling arms. She was in a curious position, almost as if she had been thrown there. Stuck in the strands of hair was seaweed, not yet dry. The body was bloated, with little holes in the skin, her nice shape distorted in gruesome self-parody. She had been in the water a while before taking this ride.

"Lady Godiva herself," I said.

"More like lady go die," Velda said, in hushed horror.

The chief came over. This time he was remarkably civil. "What do you make of it, Mr. Hammer?"

I shrugged. "Mind if I have a better look?"

Chiefie made a gracious "after you" gesture. "We're fortunate to have a big city investigator like you here to give an opinion."

There was no sarcasm apparent in that, and you would think our earlier meeting had been filled with back slapping and laughter.

"Glad to," I said, and approached Godiva.

With a stick I eased her hair aside. The chief was right beside me and I directed his attention to her neck. Imprinted there were the unmistakable marks of fingers, blotches that were bluish with deep ridges in the flesh where the fingernails had bitten into it.

"Choked to death," I commented. "Sure as hell."

"Obviously," the chief said. "Then she was thrown into the water."

"Right. Where she stayed for a while. Question is— what's she doing here?"

The chief appeared puzzled. "I don't know, Mr. Hammer. But we'll get to the bottom of it, never fear."

I managed not to laugh. I keep a straight face when I said, "If I can be of help, don't hesitate."

"I appreciate that, Mr. Hammer. Perhaps… perhaps we got off on the wrong foot."

This time I couldn't stop the laugh. "Yeah, perhaps."

Somebody called, "Chief Beales! Come here, please."

Chiefie walked over to Mayor Holden and they conversed in low tones. Holden was damn worried, that much was apparent.

Velda had my arm. "What could the motive be?"

"Show me that," I said, "and I show you the killer."

Despite a sad expression, Velda regarded the dead woman in a manner as business-like as mine. "Gone about a week, I'd say."

"Me, too, but we can't be sure. If we're right, though, she'd have been killed just about the time she disappeared. Come on, kitten."

"Where are we going?"

"To get the jump on these dumb hicks."

CHAPTER FOUR

We stopped first at the telegraph office. On a blank form, addressed to Pat at his home, I wrote: CASE HISTORY CLOSED ON SUBJECT OF OUR DISCUSSION. That was in the event the Western Union clerk was another of Holden's snoopers. I didn't want His Honor to know I had already contacted the city police about this.

When I finished, I had to wait a while for Velda to come out of a pay booth outside the office. She was making call after call. What was she up to?

I asked her who she'd been phoning, and she said, "The papers."

"The New York City papers?"

She nodded and said, "Sharron Wesley maintained a New York residence, too, and after that trial of hers, ought to still make good copy. Besides, letting the newsboys in on it right away will only put us in solid with them."

I gave that the horse laugh. "Me in solid with those jackals? They'd pimp their Aunt Hattie for a headline. You know how they smear me whenever they can, and—"

She touched my sleeve. "Mike, let's use *them* for a change."

I thought about it, then shrugged. "What the hell, let them in on it. If nothing else, it'll put a bug up the tail of the local PD."

"And Mayor Holden. When are you going to get around to giving him a little attention?"

"That'll come."

I guided Velda out to my heap just as dusk was turning to dark. We got in and headed for the hotel.

"You stake out a stool in the bar and keep an eye out," I told her. "It won't take those reporters long to drive out from the city."

"Roger."

I checked my watch. "It's ten after seven now. They'll be here by ten."

"Or sooner, if any of them charter a private plane. There's an airport about fifteen miles from here."

I nodded. "They'll swarm over Beales and his boys, and when they come back with their stories, see if you can find out when that body was placed on the horse. From the dampness of the corpse, the stuff in her hair, I'd say she wasn't there a full hour before we arrived."

"That would be my guess, too."

"Hey, maybe our friend the coroner could narrow it down for us. Call Doc Moody and see if you can wrangle a more approximate time of death out of him. It may be necessary to wait for an autopsy, but get what you can."

"Okay."

"It's possible that there was somebody hanging around the park. If anybody's been taken into custody, find out who. That's something the reporters would pick up on."

I pulled up in front of the hotel.

"So," she said, "that's what *I'm* doing. What about you,

big boy? Where are *you* going?"

"Out."

"Out. That mysterious place where all men go off to. Go on—leave me in the dark. That's where I do some of my best work."

I wouldn't mind getting some first-hand experience on that score.

"All right, baby, all right. First I'm going to the Wesley place, then out to see Poochie. He's had some recovery time and might be ripe for further questioning. I may need you in a hurry, so be where I can reach you."

"Okay, Mike, I'll behave. If I'm not in the bar, I'm in my room. And listen… watch yourself out there."

"Quit your worrying."

"I can't help it. You're strictly a city boy and this is the wilderness. If this case was in the tenement district, I'd feel a lot better, but when it comes to trees and grass, you're strictly the proverbial fish out of water."

I leaned over and kissed her, quick but sweet.

"You're cute," I said. "Now do what I told you. It's not like I'm out hunting Indians."

She gave me a look, said, "Then try not to come back with an arrow between your ears," and hipped it inside the hotel.

I drove down the highway to the cutoff that led to the Wesley house. I found it after passing by twice, then had to unlatch an iron gate to drive in. I didn't go the full length of the driveway, but stopped with the house in sight and slid the jalopy up against some bushes to one side. I hadn't had my lights on, and the motor was practically silent, so if there was anyone here, they hadn't heard me coming.

I got an extra .45 clip from the glove compartment for my left-hand suit coat pocket, and also a flashlight.

When I hopped out, I checked my rod, then started up the path, staying on the grass to muffle my footsteps. The path curved out into a wide semi-circle that swept in front of an oversized veranda. For a long moment I just stood there. The moon came out and lit the place up in a pale greenish light, accentuating its lines with long shadowy fingers.

On my left was a newer section, obviously built on in recent years. I chose that first and clung to the shadows as I made my way toward it. The new part turned out to be a free-standing garage. But what a garage.

When I lifted the roll-type door, I guided the beam of the flash around inside like I was bringing in small aircraft. The place was big enough for a fleet of taxis. The concrete floor was well-splotched with oil and grease stains, with the skid marks of countless wheels in the dust.

A nifty '45 convertible Caddy stood light-blue and lonely in a far corner. I stepped over oil puddles to the big beautiful buggy and worked the flash over her chassis. On the driver's door were the cursive initials, "S.W."

Sharron's personal ride.

Well, she wouldn't be using it now.

I looked inside. The interior was showroom clean, and the glove compartment was filled with the usual road maps, plus one item of interest—a set of car keys. Wasn't *that* an invitation to dine. Too bad Velda's boss was an honest sort, or she might have been driven back to Manhattan in style...

Only the trunk key didn't work. I tried the ignition to see if these keys were to another vehicle, but the motor purred to life. I shut it quickly off and returned to the trunk. Its lock yielded to the fourth pair of picks I tried. That trick came in handy—the technique and the picks were given to me by a little shrimp of a second-story man for whom I had gotten a real job and set straight.

A spare tire lay under the sheet of flooring with the handle of a bumper jack sticking out alongside it. Above it was a tool kit and a cardboard box about the size of a portable record player. With a screwdriver from the kit, I pried through the corrugated top and pulled the newspaper wrapping off.

Chips.

A whole damn box swimming with poker chips, white, blue, red. Was this the precious cargo that made changing that lock worth doing?

I slapped the cover back on, wiped any prints off it, and closed the trunk. Let the local cops open it themselves. They'd probably use a fire ax, knowing their finesse.

Back out in the cool, breezy evening, with the rush of tide as a soundtrack, I took the long way around the garage and found a rear door up three cement steps.

This time I didn't need the picks. It was unlocked, but I pushed it open an inch and felt for wires. There were alarm devices that depended on a door being opened six or eight inches before they went off, a neat trap for doors that could be easily forced, and I didn't feel like getting caught with my pants down. Beales and Dekkert would just love to have an actual charge to slap against me.

Nothing.

I let it open another inch and ran my fingers inside between the hinges. No wires here, either. Just as I was about to throw the door open all the way, I stopped and felt under the lower hinge. A spring attachment caught under my fingernail.

Using my left hand to shield the beam of the flash, I let a stream of light shoot through the crack of the door and pried the spring away with the largest of the picks. Needed to use a pick after all, but it only took a second.

The thing jumped out of place and I killed the flash and shoved the door open.

I stood still as death but heard no sound from anywhere—even the night noises had stayed outside. I quieted my own breathing and felt in front of me. A few minutes more and my eyes became accustomed to the darkness and I could see the outline of things pretty well. The moonlight, coming in the windows, helped.

I was in the kitchen, a big one, white and clean with enough cabinets and counters and stove tops to feed a small army. I played statue for a good, long minute. A house this size could easily have some live-in servants and I didn't want them breaking up my party.

There was nothing of interest in the kitchen, as far as I could see. Nothing I was looking for, but *what* was I looking for? I didn't know. Sharron Wesley was dead, and she had left behind a corpse on a stone horse, and this mansion. But she was murdered and that hadn't been without purpose. Whatever the reason, there might possibly be a tie-in with something within these walls. Something, anything at all. Just one thing out of the ordinary.

The room off the kitchen was a pantry. I didn't waste time there either, but stepped through the open door to what should have been a dining room. It probably had been, at one time, but not now.

Now? Now the room was a giant gambling den— taking up more space than just the dining room had once, with walls clearly torn out to make it more expansive. I've seen plenty such layouts in my time, but this one took the cake. I let my flash try for the walls, but it had to cover sixty feet before it did. That was the width. The room ran along the whole waterfront section of the house, a full hundred and fifty feet.

Overall, it had any gambling joint in the city shaded. I took my hand off the light and let the unshielded beam play over the tables. Sharron Wesley had sunk a fortune into this operation. The tables had Chicago trademarks, the best money could buy. Craps tables stood along the west wall, flanked by numerous roulette wheels and cages.

There were six faro layouts and assorted poker tables with automatic card-shuffling machines built in. I threaded my way through to where six rows of slot machines were huddled in the corner, all two-bit jobs, the jackpots still full.

On each end, and in the middle, were the banks. They were built like movie cashier booths, with one exception: the glass partitions were an inch thick. Behind the opening where the money and chips changed hands, a piece of heavy steel was inlaid into the counter. Any dough that went out had to be passed around it. The thing was practically foolproof. The Wesley dame had taken no chances on being stuck up. The cashier could stay behind there without a worry—no bullet would get through that glass, and neither could the door be opened. A time lock arrangement took care of that.

The dial of the lock registered "open." I pulled on the steel door and it swung out. Inside was a telephone, a stool, a huge money drawer, a container for chips and, on the floor, a handkerchief. The drawer was empty. I picked up the tiny frilly hanky and took a close look at it. In one corner was the initial "G," and the thing still held the faint, musky aroma of expensive perfume.

With the handkerchief, I picked up the phone to see if it was alive. A buzz came from the receiver so I cradled it. I backed out of the booth and stuck the handkerchief in my side pocket. I couldn't see what good the thing would do me, but you never can tell.

A dusty smell was in the air, not the smell of disuse, but

that of a place not recently cleaned. The protective covers of the tables were covered with a fine coating of dust and sand particles. Not much, but just about as much as would settle in a week.

This place was certainly no amateur joint, nor was it the indulgence of a rich man's whim, or rich woman, either. This nifty little casino had every hallmark of the real thing. Those wild parties in Sidon I had heard rumors about were juicy orgies of gambling.

This house was run for one reason—to make money. But why, I couldn't figure. Sharron Wesley had supposedly inherited a cool million or more from her late husband.

A hard-living dame like that ex-chorine could go through money fast enough, that was a cinch, but a million is a lot to spend and she hadn't had that much time yet. Still, I guessed there was no reason why she shouldn't go into business for herself, to keep afloat among the money set.

Oh, hell, *that* idea was out the window—that bimbo didn't have enough brains in her yellow-haired head to put together a sophisticated gambling operation like this one on her own steam.

Somebody had been backing her.

The darkened opening of a foyer led from the casino area. I looked in, then—through the archway on one side—spying the bar, a big horseshoe-shaped affair. *Damn!* This lodge-type area alone could accommodate a few hundred at a sitting. Sharron Wesley had been no piker when she built this indoor amusement park.

Stools were arranged in orderly fashion around the bar with tables-for-two set against the wall. The whole place had been swept and put in order after the last party, which hadn't been so long ago, either. You'd think a place like this would be put in for the summer crowd, but that didn't seem to be the case. This was a year-round operation that must have catered strictly to the city slicks who came out to throw their dough around, and away.

Under the bar, I found a bottle of Scotch, removed the cork and took a short pull. Good stuff. I put the cork and the bottle back. The walls in this place had been finished in knotty pine, giving the room a healthy outdoor odor. I made my way completely around the bar, then took the foyer to the side door.

A cloakroom was built into the wall with enough hangers for the Stork Club and then some. Next to the cloakroom was a second-floor staircase. I shone the light on the steps—they, too, were dust-covered. So much for servants. If anyone was up there, they must be hibernating. No one had used the staircase in a week, at least.

Nevertheless, I took no chances. I judged the approximate number of steps to the top and went up, walking as close to the bannister as I could, to avoid letting any telltale squeaks announce my presence.

The top landing was covered by a Chinese rug thick enough to muffle any sound. The corridor led to one main room that occupied half the entire upper floor—a ballroom. A stage that could have accommodated Glenn Miller's band took up the far end, and a fully functioning bar ran along one wall, while a sea of little round tables with chairs surrounded a waxed and polished beach of hardwood, a dance floor larger than the usual night club variety.

The other rooms were bedrooms. No one lived in them—they seemed to be designed to provide couples with a comfy trysting option; or maybe high-end prostitution was part of the party fare Sharron Wesley offered. At one end of the hall was a three-room apartment. This was the first place that looked well used. A glamorous, silver-framed portrait of Sharron was displayed on a baby grand. Around it were a dozen smaller framed photos, all of men.

These had been Sharron's quarters, all right.

It was beginning to dawn on me how she operated. She lived here, but she lived alone. And while this apartment was nice enough, it was bizarre to think that the wealthy widow of E.J. Wesley existed in only three fairly small rooms in her own lavish mansion. This was how the help lived, at least they did if their rich boss wasn't a bastard.

Nowhere in the well-appointed but relatively small apartment could I find evidence of male occupation, which wasn't like her at all. None of those guys with their pictures on the baby grand had toothbrush and pajama privileges. Nor could I find any servant's quarters. Whenever Mrs. Wesley gave a shindig, she must have imported a full staff of servants from the city to do the arranging and the cleaning up.

The guest list must have been a carefully selected bunch. If they weren't, news of this joint most certainly would have found its way to county or state officials and there would have been hell to pay. Admittance then, would be by invitation only, a swell way to attract the suckers and snobs. Very hush hush or you were kicked out on your well-off fanny, maybe worse. If they did squawk, they'd only leave themselves open for a gambling charge.

Neat.

I opened a few drawers and poked around a bit, but there was nothing of unusual interest. After completing a tour of the rooms, I walked downstairs and around to the new kitchen to complete the circuit. I had my eyes open all the way and I know where to look, but I never found what I wanted.

In that whole damn house there wasn't one sign of a safe.

I had looked in all the usual places and unusual, as

well, behind pictures, under desks, checking for loose carpet. No safe.

If Sharron Wesley didn't have one in the house, she must have buried it somewhere on the property. One thing was certain, money wasn't being banked or stored where a check could be kept and income tax dragged out of it. An illegal den like this didn't dare operate that way. There was the likelihood that she had a partner in the venture, and he hauled the dough back to the city. But the parties were probably Friday/Saturday affairs. And I doubted a bank run would happen daily, eighty miles out on Long Island like this. A Nassau County bank, perhaps, but that was still a drive. Any operation like this needed a safe for overnight purposes, at least, and I could not find one.

It was past eight-thirty and I still had to see Poochie—a guy like him could be in the rack already. Living as close to the Wesley mansion as he did, it was highly probable that he had witnessed plenty of the goings-on out here that the townspeople didn't know about... and I wanted to see him before the cops tried to question him again, in the wake of Sharron Wesley's Godiva act.

Now that they had something besides a disappearance to go on, the Sidon PD had a legitimate reason to drag Poochie in to answer a few questions, and knowing their interrogation techniques, I wanted the little guy left strictly alone.

I went out a side door. The same flagstone path that I had seen from the shore took me past the gazebo to the beach and I hit the sand for the walk to the shack.

In the moonlight, the little structure was just a dark blot on the beach. No light was on. The water lapped softly on the sand, and at regular intervals the hooting of some night bird broke the oppressive stillness. Overhead the moon skidded behind a cloud, but a few stars winked off and on like a street sign.

When I was still fifty feet away, an ominous snarling came from Poochie's hut, then a higher-pitched growl, almost trying for harmony. His cats. They lived outside the shack, huddled like feline watchdogs. They spit repeatedly at the night, then a lantern flared up within the hovel and there was a banging as the occupant shut his door. Then the metal clank of a bolt shot into place.

"It's *me*, Poochie," I called out as I approached. "It's Mike!"

No answer. I went up to the door and knocked.

"Who... who is it?" His voice was high and frightened. He lacked the confidence of his cats.

I was about to respond when a furry body flung itself at my legs and nails ripped through my pant leg into the flesh. I let out a curse and detached the cat from my leg and yelled, "*Ow!*"

The bolt went back and the handmade door opened. "Mike! Gee, I *thought* it was you, but I wasn't sure. Here, let me take the naughty kitty cats off your hands."

"They're not on my hands, pal, they're on my legs!"

Poochie bent down and took one animal from around my feet and called for the other. When he spoke to the creatures, telling them I was a guest and to be nice, their tails went down and they treated me like an old friend, rubbing against my legs and purring. That was well and good, but my trousers were still ripped.

Poochie had the remnants of a bathrobe flung over his shoulders and one hand held his pants up. The table was still littered with shell carvings and the remains of a fish supper. He brought the lamp over and set it on the table.

He bit his lower lip, and looked at me like a scared child. "The cops, Mike? Will they come back?"

"They might."

"Oh, Mike. Why do they wanna hit me all the time for? Don't let 'em drag me down that alley again, *please*…"

"They won't. Don't worry." I tried to be reassuring, even if I knew he really did still have those bastards to contend with. I would do my best to protect him, and intimidate them into leaving him alone, but he remained at risk.

"Gee, Mike, that's swell to hear. You're good to me. You're the only guy around here that is. Just one other guy that ever does nice things for me, you know who?"

"No, who?"

"Big Steve. He gives me meat for my cats. Plenty of meat."

"Big Steve is all right."

"Oh, you *know* Big Steve!" Poochie grinned. "He says they're leftovers, but they ain't, and he gives me so much food, the cats won't eat it all and I end up eating most of it. I like Big Steve, too… but not as much as I like you, Mike."

The over-age kid was so damn frank he made me sweat.

"How long you lived around here, Poochie?"

"Gosh, Mike, a long time."

"Yeah, but how long?"

He looked pained and squirmed in his seat. Twice he squinted at me, but said nothing.

"Can't you remember?" I asked him.

He shook his head sadly. "I can't hardly remember nothing sometimes. Only when my head hurts do I remember things. Mike, what's the *matter* with my head? I heard a man say once I was crazy. *Am* I crazy? The guy that sells bait on the barge is crazy, but I ain't like him. He spits on himself and don't even know where he lives sometimes, but I ain't that bad. I just can't remember things hardly. Only when my head hurts."

"When your head hurts, what do you remember?"

He shrugged and gave me a tight grin as though he thought the idea of it was pretty funny himself. "I dunno. I just remember stuff… when my head hurts."

"You remember your name? Not 'Poochie,' but your real name?"

"Uh-huh. Stanley Cootz. Stanley Cootz. Stanley Cootz. I say it over and over, 'cause I can't always remember it. You asked me fast-like, and I told you. I ain't crazy, am I, Mike?"

"Naw, any guy that tells you that is nuts himself. Lots of people can't remember things. Hell, sometimes I have nights where the next day I can't remember a goddamn thing."

"You shouldn't say bad words, Mike."

"I know I shouldn't, Pooch. I'm sorry. Tell me something. You don't need your head to hurt to remember that lady with the yellow hair, do you?"

"Oh, no! I remember her all right. That wasn't long enough ago not to remember. I didn't like her. She was not a nice lady and—"

"She's dead, Poochie," I cut in.

He stopped short and his head jerked around. "Dead?" It was like the word had no meaning to him.

I nodded. "Somebody killed her. Murdered her."

"Murder…"

"Choked her, then threw her in the ocean."

Poochie frowned and his chin crinkled, his eyes growing damp. "Ooooh. That's too bad. She wasn't a nice lady, but nobody should have done that to her. Who done it, Mike?"

"I don't know, Poochie. But maybe you can tell me."

His eyes widened, terror replacing sorrow. "But *I* didn't do it, Mike! *I* don't kill people." Tears flowed down his stubbly cheeks and his mouth quivered.

"I know you didn't. Now stop that."

He nodded, swallowed, rubbing his eyes with the tattered sleeve of his robe and sniffling.

"It's just that you may have seen something important. Something that could lead me to the yellow-haired lady's killer. Now think back, Poochie. Think back about a week ago. Did you see the lady then?"

"A week ago?"

"A week ago."

"I… I *think* I saw her."

"Think you saw her?"

"I saw her… but I didn't do nothing!"

"Who was she with?"

"Her dog."

"Nobody else?"

"Nope. Just her dog. It's a big boxer dog. Bothers my cats sometimes."

"Okay. What was she doing?"

"Just walking with the dog. Then she saw me and said some bad words. Worse words than you said, Mike. Then she was throwing clam shells and sticks at me, so I ran away and ran inside my house and shut the door so she couldn't come in. I took my cats in so that mean dog wouldn't bother them, either. She was right outside there." He pointed past me to his door. "She said some more bad words, and went away."

"And that was the last time you saw her?"

His head bobbed on his skinny neck, assenting.

"Poochie, did you ever see the parties at the house?"

"Oh, sure. They threw away lots of good stuff that I found. Look." He pulled a cardboard box of chipped crockery from under the table. "I'm saving them for when I have company. Ain't they nice, Mike?"

"Swell. Tell me about the parties. Can you remember those pretty well?"

He was nodding, smiling. This was a memory he liked. "Yeah, I remember them because I got so much to eat.

Lots of cars come in there, and when you stand up close to the house, you can hear the music. Sometimes when the door opens, the music gets real loud."

From that I took it that the house must be partially soundproofed.

I asked, "Were there many lights on?"

"Naw, not so many. It was hard to see on account of them shutters that was closed all the time. Guys used to give me dimes for helping 'em push out cars what was stuck in the sand. Sometimes I was too weak and they would let me sit behind the wheel and they would push." His eyes brightened. "One give a *dollar* once!"

Big shots. Spend a fortune gambling and throw peanuts to the little moron. But Poochie didn't care. He thought they were doing him a favor.

"Did you ever see any fights on the grounds? Maybe down on the beach?"

"No, not really. I saw a lady slap a guy once, though. They were in the bushes by the little house. They was wrestling, I think."

That was a new name for it. I had to stop and think what to ask him next. Getting information out of this character was like trying to hold onto a wet eel.

"How often did the yellow-haired lady have parties, Poochie?"

"Oh, lots of times. Always on the same days."

"When was that?"

"Oh, that was the days when the red bus goes past. I can tell that way."

The red bus he mentioned was the area transit company's weekend morning runs to Wilcox, the nearest town of any large size. It went by every Friday and Saturday morning about nine o'clock. I'd made the trip once myself, the last time I'd visited Sidon.

"Now think real hard, Poochie. Did you ever see anyone around there that really sticks in your memory? Somebody you might have seen before?"

A quick flash of fear passed over his face and he shrank back a little.

I pressed him. "Tell me, Poochie—did you?"

His head shook nervously. "No, Mike, don't make me tell you things like that. I don't want to get hit again."

Again.

"Was it Dekkert you saw?"

He chewed on his lip and fell silent. He shrugged. Maybe he had forgotten the guy's name.

"You know," I insisted, "Dekkert—the deputy chief?"

"Yes, yes, Mike, I did see him there… but you won't tell on me, will you? He'll hit me again. I know he will."

"Don't you worry," I assured him. "If Dekkert tries anything, I'll knock his block off. Whatever you tell me is just between us pals, Poochie."

The beachcomber was really jumpy now. He only knew that someone was dead, and that nobody around here liked him, and that he was liable to get throttled if he said too much.

Gently I said, "Now, just tell me when you saw him."

The little guy was shaking his head, almost frantically. "He's there all the time, Mike. At that place. When lots of people come, he always comes too. He caught me at the garbage cans one time, when I was looking for meat for my cats. He hit me, a bunch of times, and he woulda hit me more, only some lady yelled at him from a car and he just told me to get the heh… to get out of there."

"At the yellow-haired lady's place, Pooch… was he always outside?"

I figured Dekkert for doing security and helping cars get parked.

"*Not* just outside. I watched out for him, 'cause I didn't wanna get hit, but I guess he was inside most of the time. I stayed in the bushes so he wouldn't see me, but I always saw him, coming out the door where the garbage cans are. He came out sometimes and went down to the little place with some men."

"Little place?"

"By the trees. That little house."

The gazebo.

I asked, "Did you follow him? Did you ever hear what they spoke about?"

Poochie shook his head slowly. "No *sir*, not me. I never went *near* 'em."

Well, that was that. The gist of it seemed to be that Dekkert was there strictly as a strong-arm. He'd be good at that. I wondered if those little sojourns to the gazebo were to put the squeeze on a welcher. Nice out-of-the-way place for it.

And it was no wonder that the cops had started beating the bushes for Sharron Wesley a week after her vanishing act—without her around, there'd be no regular weekend "party" out at that ocean-side casino. Maybe Dekkert was interested in Sharron's sudden departure because, as his employer, she owed him some cash.

It was later than I thought. I slapped my hat back on and was about to say good night to Poochie, but I never got that far. His mouth was open and his tongue fell loosely over his bottom lip. But his eyes were as glassy as beads and focusing over my shoulder.

"*Mike!*" he blurted.

Poochie's skinny frame hit me before I could move.

There was a smashing roar in the room and the acrid fumes of cordite blasted at me.

CHAPTER FIVE

We hit the floor together.

My head connected hard with the edge of a crate on the way down and I could feel my eyes film. For a few seconds tiny particles of fire burned my cheek, then the whole side of my face felt as if it were lying in a brazier of hot coals. I pushed Poochie's limp form from me and fought my way to my feet.

The shot had come through the pane-less window. I yanked the .45 from under my shoulder, thumbed off the safety, kicked the slide back. I threw the shack's crude door open and dashed outside.

The beach was deserted.

No overt sounds interrupted a silence that wasn't really silence at all, wind whispering over sand, waves lapping, trees rustling, my watch ticking. A motorboat, not close enough to have carried away the assailant, put-putted along, no telling how far out, the way wind carried sound on the water.

The moon showed me footprints in the sand by the window, but they led to the line of trees up and back, behind the shack. Where the sand gave way to grassy land, I bent down and laid my ear to the ground. Somebody was running, running hard. Very faintly, I picked up the footsteps, but they grew steadily fainter and died out altogether.

He was gone.

The bastard.

Holstering the .45, I ran back to the shack. Poochie was prostrate on the floor, blood seeping through his shabby robe. I ripped away the t-shirt beneath and examined the wound. It was high up against his neck. The bullet had gone through cleanly, not touching the bone, missing the jugular vein by a hair.

I pulled a handkerchief from my hip pocket and tore it in half, then made a compress of each section and pressed it to the openings of the hole. I tore off the tail of my shirt and tied it around his neck to hold the compresses in place.

Poochie's eyes flickered once. He smiled, and passed out again. The little dope had tried to take that bullet for me. He had deliberately thrown himself in front of me to save my life. By God, from now on he was going to stay under my wing.

And if he died somebody was going to leave this world screaming with a broken back.

He was light as a feather in my arms. I cradled him as gently as I could and half-ran to the Wesley house. By the time I reached the car, I was panting heavily. That trek through the sand had taken it out of me. I gently rested Poochie down in the passenger's seat, then got behind the wheel and backed out of the driveway and took off for town like a bat out of hell.

That heap of mine was a pre-war number that looked like nothing but was really something, with good rubber and a souped-up engine. Trees blew by like a giant picket fence as I cut down the middle of a highway that was all mine, hitting one hundred by the time the modest twinkling of lights announced Sidon.

I went through the city with my hand on the horn. Parked cars glared at me with the reflection of my brights in their unlit headlamps as I swept by. A few lights were on and there was a small crowd stuffed in Big Steve's place—probably reporters. In front of the grocery I braked to a stop. The two floors above the grocery were Dr. Moody's office and living quarters. I hoped my old drinking buddy wasn't on a Saturday night bender.

But Dr. Moody opened the door, looking crisp and alert in what was likely his one and only suit. As the coroner, he'd had to inspect Sharron Wesley's corpse and he was still dressed for the occasion. His eyes flared at the sight of the little guy I had carried up two flights like Daddy conveying a slumbering child to a bedroom.

"What have you got there, Mike?"

"Gunshot wound. Where'll I put him?"

Moody led us back down a flight to his offices on the second floor, unlocking the door quickly as I carried the unconscious Poochie into a small waiting room, ancient but clean. The doc pointed to a door, which he opened for us, and I lugged Poochie in. The examining room was done up as well as any hospital's, and just as completely. The old boy may have been a drunkard, but he still knew his stuff.

As gently as possible, I laid the unmoving form down on the examining table with its crisp white paper. Moody was washing his hands at a gleaming sink. When he finished, he came over and unfastened the crude bandages I had applied and inspected the wound.

I asked, "How does it look?"

"He'll live."

"I like the sound of that diagnosis."

"Maybe so, but little Poochie here came really close to cashing in. We've graduated from a severe beating to a nearly fatal gunshot wound. What the hell happened *this* time?"

As I told him, Moody cleansed and dressed the wound. Together we got Poochie out of his rags down to his skivvies and slid him into a white gown. The doc cranked the examining table into a prone position and made sure his unconscious patient had his head comfortably positioned. The little guy was still out. I guess the shock of it was too much for him.

Moody crooked his finger for me to follow him, and I did, back out into the waiting room. We took a couple of chairs and I scooted mine to face him.

"Mike, you'll have to leave him here with me for a few days."

I gave him a quick look. "Why, Doc? It's a clean wound—in and out."

"Infection. That and shock are real possibilities. I know Poochie pretty well, and his habits, from eating to exercise, aren't conducive to good health—his kind doesn't have much resistance to this sort of thing. He's little more than a hobo, Mike."

"He makes his way in the world okay."

"Yes he does, under normal conditions. But right now, no—he'll be better off where I can keep an eye on him."

"Listen, Doc," I said, "somebody took a shot at me and that little guy stepped in front of it—stepped *into* it—purposely. I owe him. He saved my life, and if anything happens to him, I'll rip this lousy town wide open."

Moody was raising his hands in surrender. "Nothing will happen."

"You don't get it yet, Doc. Some bastard tried to murder me… and Poochie was staring at the window at the time. He *saw* who did it… and I want him to be able to talk."

Moody sighed, thought that over. Then he prescribed me a cigarette and I took him up on it.

We lit up.

"You know, Mike," he began, "I am fully aware of the deplorable conditions in this town. As a doctor, I have the questionable distinction of being connected with the so-called local legal system as police coroner. However, that service is rendered by me purely as a protective measure."

He pulled heavily on his cigarette and blew a cloud of smoke toward the ceiling and continued.

"I was a good doctor once," he said. "I had a fine practice and a family, over in Wilcox… but I lost that family at one blow. It happened when our car overturned while coming home from a trip. From then on I went to pieces. I began drinking, realizing the consequences that would follow, but not caring. Naturally, my practice dropped off. Before I went completely to pot, I moved to Sidon with all my equipment. The police coroners offered me the post and I took it so that, in any event, I would still have an income. As the only doctor, I do have a small practice here in town. I've been careful to limit my self-sedation to off-hours. I can honestly say I have never endangered any patient's life with my… weakness."

"So what do you think of the local law, and the angles they play?"

"They stink—the cops and their angles. You've been here enough times, Mike, to know that the town operates solely for the profits it derives from its summer visitors. As long as the political system assists the local populace in getting the almighty dollar, a populace that overlooks the methods practiced in doing so, they keep the system in place and intact. Of course, by now the system has its hooks so far into the people that they have to vote a certain way, to protect their own interests."

"I figured that out in about fifteen seconds. What about Sharron Wesley? How does she figure? Or I should say, how *did* she?"

Moody squinted at me curiously. "How much do you know about her?"

"Just about everything," I told him.

Maybe I was making a mistake, admitting that. Moody's disapproval of the local "system" didn't lessen his obligation to the dirty cops and corrupt public officials who provided him with a pay check.

But so what if anything got back to those sons of bitches? If I was stepping on toes, I didn't give a damn. I'd just as soon smash every goddamn toe in that system Moody complained about. There was nothing that I had to lose, and if they felt like playing rough, they were walking right up my alley in the dark.

Where I'd be waiting for them.

Unexpectedly, Moody said, "Mrs. Wesley put that mansion of hers at the disposal of certain influences and operated it as an all year-round gambling house."

"Certain influences? Such as?"

He smiled at me, the eyes behind the wire-rim glasses surprisingly bright. But then so was his drink-veined nose. "That I don't know, Mike. I'm sure it wasn't anyone here in town."

"Hell, don't tell me that Mayor Holden and the cops weren't in on it! Those guys are chiselers from way back."

"Oh, our glorious mayor and Chief Beales and his corrupt crew, they all have an interest all right... or had.

Don't underestimate Holden—he looks like a smalltime burgomaster, but he is one shrewd article. You can be sure that a nice slice of the profits line his pockets too."

I grunted a laugh. "That's putting it mildly. I'd be willing to bet that if the proceeds of Sharron Wesley's indoor playground were matched against the town's yearly take, it would make the legitimate stuff look like a drop in the bucket."

The doctor said nothing. He snubbed the butt out in a tray built into the waiting-room chair. Then he closed his eyes. He sat that way for damn near a minute, and then finally opened his eyes and stared at me. They had a twinkly cast now.

"You're a very impetuous person, Mike. Like everybody in Sidon, I read a New York City paper or two, and your… exploits, shall we call them… have made you a celebrity of sorts, and a notorious character. So naturally, what you've done so far on your Sidon 'getaway' is all over town. I won't say I disapprove of your activities, either. In fact, I'd like to help you. I'm not that far gone as a dipso. What is your next step?"

"Ha." I grinned at him. "That depends on a lot of things, Doc. Are you really serious about helping me?"

"Quite."

"Swell. The first thing you can do is, forget about reporting this gunshot wound."

Moody nodded.

"You have a nurse that comes in?"

He nodded again.

"Well, she and nobody is to know you have a temporary roommate in Poochie. Keep him in your private apartment, and don't let him stick his head out a window, much less hike back to that shack of his. Tell him his cats'll do fine for a couple days."

"All right."

"And when he comes to, let me know."

Another nod.

"Now," I said, "the other thing you can do is give me the inside dope on Sharron Wesley's death. The coroner eye-view."

He sighed. "Very well. Death by strangulation—I'd say about a week ago—with the body immediately thrown into the water. Somehow, she was taken from the ocean before being turned into that grotesque display in our city park."

"How do you know it was the ocean?"

He raised an eyebrow. "Salt water on her body, sand particles peculiar to this region ground into her skin, seaweed in her hair…"

I grunted an okay and he went on.

"I would estimate her body was placed on the statue about two hours from the time it was found. That's as close as I could place that—I checked the humidity with a wet bulb thermometer and computed the rate of evaporation."

Yup, the doc still knew his stuff.

He continued: "Tomorrow will be the autopsy, and I will be able to place the time of her death more closely, if you think it necessary."

"No, that's good enough, Doc. It is damn funny, though, that the corpse was reclaimed from the ocean. That's what we detectives call 'suggestive.'"

"Suggestive of what, Mike?"

"That it didn't have to be the murderer who placed Godiva's waterlogged corpse on her stone horse. That one incident has all the makings of fouling this case up."

The doc's eyes were slitted behind the lenses of his wire-rims. "Why would the killer… or for that matter, someone else... make such a display out of the Wesley woman's remains? A week later? There has to be a reason behind it, Mike. As a detective you must know that."

"Sure, there's a reason for every killing, and reasons for every aspect of any killing—only some of them are too damn complicated to figure on the spot. But it'll come to me, Doc."

He chuckled and nodded. "I'm sure it will, Mike. I'm sure it will."

I got up to go and Moody walked me to the door.

Before I left I told him, "Doc, you may be on the square with me, but I don't know that for sure. I mean no offense, but remember—if anything happens to Poochie, I'm holding you personally responsible."

"I understand," he said somberly. "You can have him back in a day or two. I can get in touch with you at the hotel?"

"Yes, but leave no messages. You talk to Velda or me, and not any hotel clerk. Actually, even if you get me or Velda, don't mention anything. Nothing about Poochie. Just say we need to talk, and I'll call you from a pay phone."

"Loose lips sink ships."

"Yeah," I said. I opened my suit coat and showed him the .45 in the speed rig, and winked. "But then so does heavy artillery."

When I got downstairs, I wiped some of the blood off the car-seat cushions and drove back to the hotel.

Velda was waiting for me in the lobby, which was otherwise almost empty.

I said, "Thought I saw reporters in Big Steve's diner."

She nodded. "They swarmed in here like locusts, then swarmed out. When they get back, maybe we can camp out in the bar and see what they've learned."

"Don't bother," I said, keeping my voice down. "I just talked to Doc Moody myself."

She glanced around. The skeletal night clerk was on duty again. He was staring at us the way a sailor on a long overdue shore leave eyes a curvy dame.

"Let's go up to my room," she said.

Like that was an invitation I'd turn down.

She steered me up the stairs and down the hall. She worked the key in the lock and I opened the door for her and closed it behind us. That was when she noticed the red stains on my coat.

The big beautiful brown eyes showed white all round. "Mike... you're *hurt*!"

She reached for me but I held her off.

"Not me. This is Poochie's blood."

"Poochie! Mike, what the hell happened?"

I told her while I cleaned the coat with water from a basin.

She listened intently. When I'd finished she said, "Then you have all the details on the Wesley woman. That's exactly what I learned."

"Where?"

"The hotel bar's pretty busy on a Saturday, even before the reporters showed. For some reason, men just like to buy me drinks and talk to me."

"Yeah, that's a tough one to figure."

"So what's next on the docket?"

"We're driving to New York tomorrow, Velda. Pat should have something for me and I want do some digging that can't be done over the phone."

This time, surprisingly, she didn't want to go with me. She was sitting on the edge of her bed. "Why not leave me here?"

"Yeah?"

"Maybe something will develop in Sidon, and it would be better if one of us was on hand."

Once Velda got her teeth into a case, she was as single-minded as a dog with a spare rib.

"You stay here in town then," I said, climbing back into my coat. "Keep a check on Moody, too."

"Don't you trust him?"

"Everybody I trust in this town is in this room. If you see Dekkert or Beales anywhere near Moody—his office and living quarters are over that grocery down from the picture show—you give me a buzz at Pat's. Try his office first, then his house."

"Roger."

"If that happens, maybe you can create a diversion yourself and keep those louses out of there."

"Okay."

I sat next to her on the bed. "You might also try dropping in to see Big Steve again. He may have the inside track on things without knowing it. Guy like him, working behind a diner counter, picks up on more than he even realizes."

She was nodding, taking it all in.

"Get the political angle in town… where these Keystone cops fit in… exactly where Holden stands… get everything and anything. It'll be fairly quiet, on a Sunday, but do what you can."

"Got it."

"I'll probably be gone before you get up in the morning. If anyone inquires for me, tell them that I'm around town somewhere. Stall 'em off."

Velda's business-like expression turned thoughtful. "Did you find the bullet that was fired at you from the shack?"

I shook my head. "No. First, I went after the shooter, with no luck, then hauled ass out of there getting Poochie to the doctor."

"Understandable."

"Anyway, that slug can wait. So far, it's been the only gun used on this case, and it could belong to anyone. Poochie had his eyes right on the window when the shot was fired, remember. I'm more interested in *his* story than tracing the bullet."

"You know darn well," Velda said with a humorless smirk, "that the little guy could never tell that story to a jury and have it believed."

I looked at her. "When I get whoever fired that bullet, kid, there won't be any jury trial."

"Mike…"

"You know how I operate. Nobody tries to kill me and gets to keep breathing."

She was shaking her head, her expression glum now. "You're just asking for trouble."

That was a laugh. "And they aren't? Don't forget that one of this outfit has already resorted to murder. If that isn't trouble, what is?"

"All right, Mike," she said, with a sigh. "Have it your own way. Just be careful."

I got up to leave, but she grabbed my coat sleeve and pulled me back onto the edge of the bed, and the springs bounced us some.

I knew what she wanted. Because I wanted it, too.

I tilted her chin with my fingers and kissed her. Just a friendly goodnight kiss, more than a peck, but not much more.

It was enough to get us started, though. It made me hungry for more, and she knew it. Before I could help myself, she was in my arms and I was crushing her to me. Her mouth was on fire, her hands behind my head holding my face to hers. She had those incredible breasts pressed against me like a threat or maybe a promise, and every fibre in my body was jumping with passion.

When it was over, she nuzzled my ear and kissed my neck lightly.

"Sleep tight," she said.

After a kiss like that, I'd be lucky if I could sleep at all.

So I went out into slumbering Sidon for a little late evening walk on what turned out to be a cool, breezy night. Every storefront was closed except a couple of bars, and I was almost surprised the sidewalks weren't literally rolled up.

It wasn't just Velda's kiss, though, that was keeping me awake and sending me out for a stroll. I had someone to call on and figured that by now the reporters would be done with him.

Mayor Rudolph Holden, if the flimsy little Sidon phone book could be trusted, lived two blocks off the business section in a red-brick turn-of-the-century two-story house. Quaint but well kept-up, with a nice well-trimmed lawn, this was the largest home I had spotted in the community. Across the street was a Baptist church that was only marginally bigger.

There were lights on downstairs, so His Honor was up. But I wasn't surprised when my two rings of his doorbell got no response. With that pack of reporters in town, who could blame him for ignoring it? So I hammered on the door and kept at it. Either Rudy would answer or the dead would wake. Either way should be interesting.

Rudy didn't answer, but it wasn't the dead, either. The woman was very much alive, slender and about fifty in a nice floral frock, and she hadn't removed her make-up though it was after nine. She was the kind of older-looking dame who could put on an air of respectability without losing her sex appeal. Unless this was the housekeeper, Rudy had done all right for himself.

Even if it was the housekeeper, he'd still done all right for himself.

"Yes?" she said, her tone impatient, letting me know she didn't appreciate being disturbed. She had nice hazel eyes and her white hair was youthfully arranged.

"Mrs. Holden?"

"Yes," she said again, even more impatient.

"I'm not a reporter, ma'am."

This seemed to take some of the starch out of her. But she said one more time, "*Yes?*"

Like, *what the hell* is *it?*

"Would you tell your husband that Mike Hammer is here to see him?"

"My husband is not home."

"Okay. If he is home, you should tell him I'm here. He'll want to see me. If he isn't home, you should tell me where I can find him. It's important. I'm a detective on the Wesley murder."

Her irritation turned to alarm, and she said, "Just a moment."

His Honor received me in his book-lined study. We sat in two comfy chairs before a fireplace that was of course unlighted. His wife had turned friendly, even gracious, and brought us sugar cookies on a plate and glasses of iced tea, which she set on a small table between her husband and me.

"Mr. Hammer," he said, and he had a warm baritone that was a little odd coming from a small-ish, almost roly-poly individual.

He was in the same short-sleeve white shirt as at the park, but had ditched the too-short tie. He had lost much of his hair, but boyish features kept him young-looking. Minus the pot belly, and plus a full head of hair, he'd have been a nice-looking man. Nice enough to catch that attractive wife, anyway.

Superficially, he seemed calm. But he was eating the cookies nervously. I had one—he had six as we spoke, sugar gathering on his chin like a frost on a winter window.

"We're lucky to have you in Sidon," he said, nibbling.

"Really? And why is that?"

"Well, a detective of your abilities. Your renown. We're a small town, and we're not well acquainted with murder."

"Murder gets acquainted with people in all kinds of towns, Your Honor. But you have Deputy Chief Dekkert to lean on, don't you? He has real big-city experience."

"Yes, Mr. Hammer, but his background is in vice."

It sure was.

"Well, I'd be glad to help," I said.

Was that how they planned to play it? Work with me, and keep an eye on what I was up to? In a pig's ass that would happen.

On the other hand, the mayor had just opened the door for me to make noises like a cop.

"Mayor Holden, what can you tell me about Sharron Wesley?"

"Call me Rudy, please. Everyone in Sidon knows everyone else, and we like it that way."

"Swell. But my question…?"

"Well, she was an upstanding citizen, of course. A respected citizen."

"Really? I understand she had a lot of wild parties out at her digs. And that her guests sometimes came roaring into town causing trouble, like cowboys after a cattle drive."

He shifted in his comfy chair. Nibbled a cookie. "Well, that certainly has elements of truth. But it's an exaggeration. We are a one-industry town, Mr. Hammer. And that industry is tourism."

"In other words, showing out-of-towners a good time."

"That's not how I'd put it, but I can't disagree."

I leaned forward and grinned at him. It was a nasty

enough grin to freeze him mid-cookie.

"Listen, Rudy. The Wesley broad was running a casino out there. I've only been here since Friday night and I already know that. So let's not pretend you don't."

"Well... again. We're a one-industry town."

I glanced around. "You and your lovely wife have a lovely home here."

"Well, uh, thank you, Mr. Hammer."

"Pretty much everything about your set-up is lovely."

"Set-up?"

"Deputy Chief Dekkert got tossed off the New York Police Department for graft, Rudy. That would make it hard for him to get hired on a lot of forces. But I think it was a gold star on his record, where Sidon was concerned."

He smiled through sugar-flecked lips. "I'm afraid I'm not following you."

"I know how these small towns operate. You have a casino on the outskirts. I was inside, I saw the lay-out, and it's big city all the way. Somebody from New York was backing Sharron Wesley's play."

He swallowed a bite of cookie. "Suppose that's true. What does it have to do with her death?"

"Probably everything. She was strangled, Rudy. Somebody would seem to be unhappy with her. I'd like to have a word or two with her silent partner. And yours."

He shook his head, smiling again, but it was a sick smile. "I'm afraid you're making an unwarranted assumption, Mr. Hammer. Much as I would like to help you, I simply don't know."

He nibbled on a cookie and I slapped it out of his hand. Then I slapped him a couple of times. He looked as startled as a guy in bed with somebody else's wife when the flashbulbs went off.

"I don't *know* the name! There *is* no name!"

His wife leaned in from the next room. "Dear? Is there a problem?"

"No! No."

"You're sure?"

I said, "He's sure," and looked at her with my nicest smile till she smiled back and went away.

Holden tried to straighten up and crawl inside the upholstery at the same time. "Are you insane, man? I'm the mayor of this town! You come into my house, uninvited, and threaten me, and rough me up?"

"I didn't rough you up. You'd know it if I roughed you up." I raised a hand in a peaceful gesture, but he jerked back, thinking I was going to slap him again. "I'm a little excitable tonight, Rudy. You see, somebody tried to kill me earlier, and I think it was your boy Dekkert."

Veins stood out on his forehead. "What? My God! What were the circumstances?"

"The circumstances were, he missed. Big mistake. You and Chief Beales and his boys need to steer clear of me, or I will treat them, and you, like the cheap crooks you are. I was just kind of curious about Sharron Wesley and why somebody would strangle her, but you know what? I didn't even like the dame. I don't approve of wholesale murder, but I don't make every killing my business. Only when I see a slobbermouth like Dekkert damn near beat to death an innocent little guy, I get annoyed. And then when somebody tries to put a bullet in my brain, I get mad."

He was shaking his head and kept on shaking it. "Mr. Hammer—I have no idea who Sharron Wesley's silent partner was. I will not deny that I had a small piece of her action. But I dealt only with *her.*"

"Interesting."

"Interesting?"

"That makes you a suspect."

I left him there with one last cookie on the plate. I thanked his wife for the iced tea and told her she had a lovely home.

She smiled, as if to say, *What a polite young man*, and showed me to the door.

CHAPTER SIX

"All right," Pat Chambers said, "go over it again."

He leaned back in his swivel chair and listened while I told the story for the third time. This captain of Homicide was careful and crafty, with an adding machine for a brain and the smooth manner of a man-about-town.

But all cop.

We were in his office off the station-house bullpen of the red-brick building where he worked, sometimes even on Sunday, like this afternoon. The place maybe was bustling a little less than on other days, but otherwise, it was business as usual.

My third recitation took longer than the last as I fitted in little details and opinions that had escaped the previous tellings. I ended with my leaving Sidon that morning, after breakfast at Big Steve's. A man has got to eat.

"You come up with a murder motive yet?" Pat asked.

"For Sharron Wesley or for me? I damn near bought it, you know."

He shrugged. "Take your pick."

I gave him a shrug back. "No definite motive. But plenty of reasons for one."

"What reasons?"

"Start with, that town is as crooked as a corkscrew. Isn't that reason enough?"

He rocked in the chair, hands locked behind his neck, elbows winged out. "I just love the way you think, Mike. So simple and direct."

"That doesn't sound like a compliment."

Now he sat forward, resting his hands on his desk and folding them, as if about to say grace. "Naturally, there's a motive and it won't be an obscure one, but based on what you've gathered so far, I'd say getting down to it will be tough. What can I do for you?"

That was the line I'd been waiting for.

"First of all," I said, and I sat forward too, "I want to see if you can get me any info on Rudy Holden. Find out if he is as innocuous as he looks and sounds. When I talked to him last night, he played dumb, but he's living in the biggest, swellest house in town filled with the kind of furniture you don't get at the Salvation Army."

Pat scribbled Holden's name down on a note pad.

I went on: "Rumor around Sidon is that he's a little guy in the bigger scheme of things... but in a small town, a little guy can be pretty goddamn big."

Pat raised a hand for me to hold it a minute, got on the phone, spoke a few words, and before he had even lowered his hand, he passed the note to a uniformed cop who scrambled in, took it, and scrambled back out.

"You realize, Mike, that I can't get too deep in this thing. If it had started here in the city, I could pull strings to work with you out there in Sidon. But unless some developments carry it back to Manhattan, you're going to have to do most of the work yourself."

"I know," I said through a yawn. "That's what I'm hoping for."

"Oh, you're a one-man cleaning crew now, I suppose?"

I patted the holstered rod under my arm. "Just me and my broom."

Pat gave me a disgusted smirk. "Then you certainly don't need *my* help."

"But I do. Anyway, there *is* a tie-up with the city. Most of the clientele at Sharron Wesley's gambling house are almost certainly New York City residents. Those kind of big spenders don't limit themselves to one or two shindigs on the weekend. They'll do plenty during the week, too."

"Granted."

"So if you hear of the vice boys pulling any raids on joints around town, try to find out if any of their high-roller arrests had at any time been patrons of Sharron's shed. How's that?"

He was rocking again. "Fair enough. I'll do what I can." An eyebrow went up. "Now, how about the potshot taken at you? You're sure it was Dekkert?"

I laughed long and loud. "Natch, chum. Who else but? That punk is laying for me."

"What are you going to do about it?"

I shrugged. "Make him sweat. Then when I get ready, I'm going to take him down. All the way. As much for what he's put poor Poochie through as for the shot he sent in my direction."

Pat looked at me very seriously and spread his hands on the desk. "How can you be so sure it was Dekkert?"

"Why shouldn't I be?"

He shook his head slowly. "You could be treading on some mighty sensitive toes here, Mike. After all, you have got yourself a reputation and not a nice one at that. You stand up in front of the wrong judge with one of your self-defense ploys…"

"That's *pleas*, Pat."

"…and you're going to take a long, hard fall. Say what you will about Dekkert—and I'll say the same and worse—but he *is* a cop."

I blew a half-hearted Bronx cheer.

"Suppose," Pat went on, "the murderer knew of your antagonism for Dekkert, and used that to remove you both? If Dekkert is *not* the murderer… and there's no reason to think he is anything but a bent small-town cop with a grudge against you… then the real murderer could kill you, and suspicion would be thrown on Dekkert. The real killer could take a shot at you and miss, safely knowing you'd go after Dekkert without looking around for anyone else."

I gave that one some thought. That adding-machine mind of Pat's again had come up with an analysis that certainly sounded logical enough. But hell, who else but Dekkert would make a sucker play like that? So far I hadn't garnered anything around Sidon that was worthwhile shooting me over, just some nosing around.

Pat knew enough to let me sit there and mull it over for a while.

Then he said, "After the body was discovered, did the police get over to Sharron Wesley's place very fast?"

"No. I drove up there immediately. Took fifteen minutes or so getting there, and I fooled around for at least half an hour. After that I was at Poochie's maybe fifteen minutes before the shot was fired at me, then I carried him back to my car. In all that time there was no sign of the gendarmes."

"Unless the guy that shot at you *was* one—like Dekkert, for example."

"Roger, pal. Now you're seeing things from my point of view. To me it looks like the local boys didn't bother going out to Sharron's, because they knew just what to expect there. According to the leads I got, the entire political regime of Sidon had their fingers in that pie."

Pat was nodding. "And they couldn't go out to that casino to investigate without risking exposure of a racket they were into up to their own necks. I get the picture."

"Yeah, well, you're a little slow, Pat, but I knew you'd catch up."

That made him laugh, and he was still grinning as he said, "Okay, Mike, I'll get some men to work on this end. Suppose I call you tomorrow and let you know what I find out."

"Fine," I said, getting up to go. "You can reach me at the Sidon Arms. If I'm not there give the message to Velda. But don't leave anything pertinent—just say I should call you back."

"Got it. The walls have ears and eyes."

"Yeah, and one of these days I'll give those walls a nice new paint job. Guess what color."

"You do know I'm a cop, right?"

We grinned at each other, shook hands, and I walked out.

I left the heap in the usual garage and walked the half block to the Hackard Building. Getting in the building required a key that only long-time tenants possessed. There was nobody manning the visitor's book on Sunday and the lobby was so dead, I was almost surprised tumbleweed wasn't blowing through.

I took the elevator up to the eighth floor where we kept a two-room suite of offices, and I was fishing out my keys when I noticed the lights on and shadows moving behind the pebbled glass that said HAMMER INVESTIGATING AGENCY.

My keys wouldn't be needed—the door was a little ajar already. I put them back in my pocket and got the .45 in my mitt and thumbed the safety off and went in fast and low.

But there were two of them, one going through the filing cabinets to the right, and that gave him the chance to hammer me on the back with clenched hands, sending me face down, hitting the wood floor hard with the rod spilling from my fingers and skittering under Velda's desk, spinning like a deadly top. Somebody clicked off the overhead lights, and with no windows in the reception area, shadows draped everything and all I could make out as I rolled onto my back were two shapes in baggy suits and hats, one at my right, coming at me with clawed fingers, and the other at the left, going through Velda's personal filing cabinet, pausing to reach under his arm and that meant a gun would soon be belching flame, and in the wrong direction. I spun to my right and with an underhanded swing jammed four stiff fingers into the belly of the guy who'd slugged me, and he folded up like a card table, only card tables don't vomit all over the floor when they go down.

The other visitor's rod was halfway out now, a revolver, and I threw myself at him, in a wild tackle that took him down, bone-jostling hard. The fingers of both my hands found his throat and his face was just a shadowy, reddening, tongue-bulging blur as I strangled him and battered his skull into the floor in fury-fueled overkill and before I could kill the bastard, I got clouted on the back of the head, maybe with a gun butt, and fell with limp, lazy, painless ease, floating down headlong into the temporary death that was unconsciousness.

* * *

When I came around, my first thought was to keep my head down, because the Japs were out there, maybe twenty yards away, just waiting for the right target to pop up like at an arcade. I would wait till somebody laid down some covering fire and then and only then I would make a break for it, fleeing from the fox hole into the jungle with a grenade ready to toss back in their goddamn laps and let those evil assholes laugh that off.

But I wasn't in the jungle. I was on the floor of my office, the reception area. The place had been given a thorough, professional shakedown—only the two drawers they'd been rifling when I'd come in were still sticking out.

Velda would make an inventory that would say whether anything had been taken, but I felt I knew what this was about.

I sat on the couch. It stunk in there. A modern art masterpiece on the floor was where the one guy had puked. My hand found the knot on the back of my skull, but my fingers carried back no blood. They could have killed me, easy, but hadn't. Absent-mindedly, I got up, knelt down like a kid looking under his bed for his missing dog and retrieved my .45.

Gun holstered, I sat back down. My head hurt but it wasn't pounding. I was lucky. And I was almost glad it had happened.

Because now I knew this led back to the city. Now I knew somebody had been called, and that somebody had sent that pair around to check up on my office and see if I left anything of interest lying around.

After I mopped up the vomit, I went into the inner office, opened some windows, and did what I'd come for originally. I called four stoolies around town and asked them what they knew about the gambling operation out on Long Island, outside little Sidon.

Nobody knew anything, but they'd poke around for me.

The headache was getting worse and I washed down half a dozen aspirin with some bourbon. Then I did what any brave, two-fisted detective would do in this situation.

I took a nap on the couch.

I woke around nine and fifteen minutes later I was down on the street, heading for the garage. But a cab cruised by and I impulsively hailed it.

I gave the driver an uptown address and settled back in the cushions. The neon-draped city certainly looked good to me. Why the hell anyone wanted to go to the sticks for a vacation was more than I could figure. Right here in Manhattan was the works—shows, bars, dancing. In Sidon, you hibernated.

Or maybe ran down a murderer.

My cab pulled up in front of a cellar bar that was stuck in the front of a boarded-up three-story building that looked ready to fall apart. The ramshackle appearance was merely a front. Behind that deteriorated stone-and-brick veneer lurked one of the city's top gambling dumps.

Louie Marone ran it. In that shady racket, he was as on the up-and-up as they came. The house took its percentage and nothing more. When you sat in a game at Louie's, you could be sure the cards weren't fixed and no wires were attached to the wheels.

Instead of steps, a ridged gangplank led to the bar and I mostly slid down it and plodded through the sawdust to the counter and parked on a stool at the end. The place wasn't hopping. Well, it was Sunday.

The bartender, a whiskered Greek right out of the Gay Nineties, quit polishing glasses long enough to set a beer up in front of me, then went back to his wiping. Besides myself, the only other occupants of the joint were a pair of rough-looking gents knocking off boiler-makers as fast as the bartender could pour. Then I noticed a pair of luscious-looking legs extending from a booth.

The legs made me curious. And I was ready to bet that the package they were part of would be just as nice as they were. This seemed to me a bet worth making, and after all, Louie was the most honest gambling joint in the city, so my odds were good.

I didn't have to reflect on my potential bet very long. A tousled head of blonde hair poked around the backrest and a very lovely body uncoiled itself from the seat and walked itself toward me. There was a lot of animal in her stride. Under the close-fitting jersey of her dress, each little muscle in her stomach and legs rippled coaxingly. If she had anything on under that thing, you could stuff it in a thimble.

She parked a glorious fanny on the stool next to me and flashed a smile in my direction.

"Why, hello, Mike," she said. She poured it out like melted butter.

Now what? I couldn't place her at all. Maybe I had taken one to the head harder than I thought...

"What do you say, kid?" I said, faking it.

"Remember me?"

I don't usually forget pretty faces, even after getting clobbered. This one belonged to a fabulous piece of fluff of about twenty-one, though she looked as though she had been around some.

"Nope," I said, deciding to keep it honest, like Louie. "Can't say I do. Not proud of it, either."

She smiled and this time it was not a come-on, but the smile of a real person, not some dame on the make.

"Marion Ruston," she said, red-nailed fingers brushing her full bosom. Lucky fingers. "Billy's little sister? I was just a kid when you got him out of that scrape that time."

Then I got it.

Billy Ruston was a kid who had started life pointed in the wrong direction. I had used him for a messenger sometimes, trying to make less of a dead-end kid out of him; but he had become involved with the law when the gang he ran with robbed a warehouse. Both Pat and I had intervened and arranged for him to join the army. Doing that, the judge had suspended sentence on him while his former pals did their stretch upstate.

Marion had been just a kid then, as she said. I remembered her crying at the trial, a pretty little flat-chested teenager. I was wondering if—like her brother—her rough background had sent her tumbling off the straight-and-narrow.

The bartender brought her a Manhattan without being asked, and I ordered up a highball.

There was a disapproving tone in my voice when I said, "What are you doing in this place?"

"A place like this? Nice girl like me?"

"Something like that, yeah."

Her mouth made a sort of smug kiss when she smiled that certain way. "Don't get me wrong, Mike. I work here."

I frowned.

"Not a B-girl! I'm Louie's bookkeeper."

I eyed the curves assembled on the stool next to me, pretending I didn't approve of them. "Then why don't you dress for the job? In that outfit…"

I let it go at that.

She laughed and it had a mocking edge. "I just like to

have a little fun, that's all. I've taken such a beating all my life, it's nice to do some pushing back myself for a change. Besides, I bring a lot a business in here."

"Doing what?"

"Being eye candy." She gave me that laugh again. "Men seem to like to look at me. I saw the way *you* looked at me, Mike, till you found out who I was."

She had me there.

"But if Louie caught me being serious with any of the goons that come in here? Why, he'd spank me but good."

If I were Louie, I'd have been looking for an excuse.

I asked, "No steady boyfriend on the outside?"

"No dice. I don't like men... not that much. I just like to tease 'em."

My highball arrived and I sipped it. "Dangerous game, honey. You're going to get caught short someday."

She shook her head and blonde curls bounced. "Not a chance. I make 'em sweat, then chase 'em home, like the scared little boys they are."

"Maybe you just haven't met the right guy."

"Get out! They're all after the same thing. Hardly a variation in technique. They put up a big show, spin a line a yard long, and then offer to show you their stamp collections."

"It used to be etchings."

"Sometimes it still is."

I was torn between my attraction to this knowing beauty and the memory of the sweet innocent kid she'd been.

"Just look out, Marion," I said softly. "Some guy is going to bust up that little game of yours, and you're going to be left holding the bag."

"Pooh."

"Some guys take a tease too serious. A girl can get manhandled."

"A guy can get kneed in the nads."

She had a point.

"Where's Louie?" I asked her.

"Upstairs," she said with a nod in that direction. "Want me to get him?"

"Do that."

Marion slid from the stool and swayed down the bar, trying a little too hard to impress me now, and disappeared into a tiny alcove. A few minutes later she was back with her boss in tow.

Louie was a big Italian with a smile for everyone, a tuxedo that dated to Prohibition, and an ardent hatred for crooks. There was nothing to say about Louie except that he was square and a swell guy, always good for a touch.

He spied me and beamed all over. "Mike! How do you do!" I never knew whether this was in imitation of the radio catch-phrase or just a greeting. "Glad to see a you. Whatcha know?"

We shook hands, and he ushered me over to a table in one corner.

A smile blossomed under a Clark Gable mustache in a J. Carrol Naish face. "What are you drinking, my friend?"

"Highball. There's plenty of this one left."

"That glass has no bottom, Mike. And your money, she's no good here."

"Thanks, Louie. How's business?"

"Good, Mike, verra good. Everybody, they spend plenty of dough. Sunday, a little slow. We have to close early, Sunday."

Right. Three a.m., instead of four a.m.

I lifted a thumb. "I mean upstairs."

"Yeah, good up there too. I spin a straight wheel. Plenty of people come to Louie's. Plenty of people, but not you, Mike. Where you been forever?"

"You know me, Louie. I'm not much of a gambler."

A grave expression took over the jovial face. "You are the great gambler, Mike. You gamble your life."

"Ah nuts," I grinned at him. "Got a few questions for you, Louie. Think you can help out?"

"Maybe so. Let's a go to my back room. Leave the glass. We can do better."

Marion, seated on a stool at the bar, saw us heading to the rear and hopped off and tagged after. She fell in just behind me.

Louie noticed, halted the procession, and gave her a long look. Then he said, "You wait out here, Marion."

"I'm with Mike."

He shook a finger at her, Daddy scolding. "This Hammer guy, he's not like them other bums. No games with him now. He'll poke you one."

She gave that ambiguous remark a short snort and threw a lush, taunting lipstick smile my direction.

"I don't think he's man enough," she said, then laughed as she walked away.

I could see where she might need a spanking at that. Later maybe.

"Little devil," Louie said, trying not to smile as he nodded toward the lithe figure. "Some a day she go too far."

"That's what I told her. You know, Louie, not all men are as gallant as I am."

He had no response to that.

The back room was a comfortable little den used exclusively to entertain Louie's prime guests between rounds of losing money. The chairs were like those in an exclusive old-time men's club—leather, studded with buttons, but very comfortable. Framed paintings adorned the walls, all winter scenes, except for a huge hand-tinted photo of the Coliseum in Rome. One corner held a cabinet lined with books, not leather-bound, but well-read volumes, from classics to bestsellers, with half a dozen books on government in the collection. You couldn't say that Louie didn't take his citizenship seriously.

Louie went to a small bar in the opposite corner, got behind it and drew out a bottle of good Scotch. He laid out two glasses and poured a stiff one in each. We held them in a mutual toast, took a long pull, and sat down facing each other, him on his side of the bar, me on mine.

"Now, wotta questions you got, Mike?"

"I got a murder on my hands, Louie. Out on the Island. A cookie named Sharron Wesley got herself knocked off. She ran a gambling joint out of a mansion she inherited."

"Yeah, I know this cookie. Didn't know she gotta bumped. I pay no attention to the papers much. When did she catch it?"

"A little over a week ago. The body was just discovered yesterday, though. I'm sure it's been in the papers here, because the reporters were thick as flies last night, and her body turned up in an unusual way."

"Oh?"

I told him about the Lady Godiva routine.

"So you think… are you saying…?" His voice was querulous. Louie was trying to see where her death had any connection with him.

I hurried to reassure him. "Wipe off the long face, pal. You're not in on this. I know that. But it so happens that you may have some customers that patronized the Wesley dame's joint, and I want to find out who they are. They could stand talking to."

He raised his palms, like the victim of a hold-up. "Mike, please. You my friend, I like a to tell you these things, but I don't want to be no pigeon. This is a my business, Mike. It is not strictly legal, I know, but it's all I got to make a dollar. Now, maybe I lose a the business if I rat."

I understood where he was coming from. But I still wanted the inside dope, and I wasn't asking him to finger any gambling bosses—just customers. Pat was sure to dig up some names for me, but it might take too long. And with bullets flying and goons shaking down my office, not to mention knocking me on my can, well… time wasn't something to be spent so leisurely.

Louie interrupted my thoughts with, "Didn't this Wesley woman leave a some books?"

"I thought of that, Louie, but the operation seems to be backed by a syndicate of a sort. If she did, you can bet your boots those ledgers are damn well hidden. I'm going to let you in on something, kiddo. This isn't to go farther than this room."

"Hokay, Mike. I keep a my mouth shut. Shoot."

Nice choice of words.

"Louie, if I'm not mistaken, there was one hell of a take from Sharron's dump. She was the one who ran the place and presumably she took care of the income. The books I'm not too worried about. It's the dough that somebody will be after. The equipment in there cost in the six-digit range—possibly seven, so you can approximate the entire take, especially if the place was crooked."

"But each week, they must a bank the take in the city."

"That casino was strictly open on weekends. She got murdered the last night of the last party, so at least that much dough may be stashed somewhere on those grounds. She may have been keeping her own share of the proceeds there, as well. If not all of it."

Louie nodded. "I catch. She stash a the cash, then a she die, now nobody knows where to look. Everybody searching for it and more people, they get bumped off. And you in the middle, making life miserable. Yeah."

I nodded. "That's how I see it. Now, here's what I can do. Either you can put me wise to a few people who make the rounds of the gambling joints, with my word it goes no farther… or I can play upstairs here a while myself on the Q.T., and snoop around. What'll it be?"

He pondered that a moment. "I a tell you, Mike. Do both."

He dragged a pad out from somewhere and unscrewed the top of a fountain pen. For a minute he wrote, then tore the sheet from the pad and handed it to me. "These are some names. I don't know where they live. You find a that out. Come here and play, watch a these people, and speak to them. Like one gambler speaks to another gambler. Just friendly. Maybe you learn something."

I thanked him and stood up.

But a voice nagged at me that this approach still would take too long, and I couldn't afford being away from Sidon any length of time. And anyway, I was well-known enough to get made.

"I'll do what I can, Louie," I said. "Maybe I'll see you tonight, upstairs."

"I'll be looking for you, Mike."

He escorted me to the mouth of the alcove and stayed behind as I headed back into the outer bar. That's when I had a swell idea, one that might prove a good shortcut.

I slid into the booth where the lovely legs had taken up residence again. On the same side as those legs, bumping their owner over.

"Just can't resist me, can you?" Marion said. Her tongue flicked out, the little snake.

I grinned at her. "Nope. You are irresistible, dolly. Like me."

She laughed once, high up. "I'm just dying to hear your approach. Is it any different than the rest of the he-men?"

"Some girls find it that way, baby. Do you have an apartment around here?"

"Sure, fifteen minutes on foot, less by cab. Why?"

"Let's go, then. We can discuss this better there."

She blinked. "What? Don't you even wanna buy me a drink first?"

"Hell no. That's such a tired come-on, right? Well? Do you want to take me home or not?"

"I should say not! What do I look like, anyway?"

"I think you know what you look like. I just thought you wouldn't mind skipping over the dull preliminaries, since you said you can take care of yourself. But if you're scared, let's forget it."

She frowned and it made her nose even cuter. "What have *I* got to be scared of… you? Don't tell me you think I took Louie's warning about you seriously. Hell, that's a laugh. There isn't a man *alive* I can't handle!"

I laughed in her face.

And that laugh hurt her. It told her that I thought she was a kid who was just kidding, and couldn't make it in the big leagues.

Marion reached up and dragged down a flimsy hat and grabbed a light coat from the back of the booth.

"Let's go, sucker," she said.

CHAPTER SEVEN

Marion Ruston's apartment was in an older building, a recently renovated brownstone. Most of the furnishings were covered in flowered chintz, very cozy, but strictly a woman's place. A man wouldn't have all the frou-frou junk she had for love nor money. I tossed my hat on a coat-tree hook and, while Marion slunk seductively into the bedroom, I stretched out in an overstuffed armchair and waited.

This should be good, I thought.

It was—in only about five minutes, she appeared poised at the hallway entry in the sheerest dressing gown imaginable. And that was all. That and red finger-and-toenail polish.

"My temptation togs," she explained with a *tah dah* hand gesture, her smile turning up at both ends.

She went over to a standing lamp to switch it off and, when she did, moved past a window where the drapes were back, letting the glow of the city at night turn her into a curvaceous silhouette. Her form had the kind of lines usual in pin-ups but unusual in life, plump firm behind, full impertinently tipped breasts, a waist you could put your hands around, and legs that followed gentle, supple curves on their way to the toes she posed provocatively upon.

"You can take that spider web off, too," I said, fishing out my deck of Luckies from my suit coat pocket, "for all I care."

As I lit up the cig, she moved toward me with a dancer's grace, and this *was* a sort of dance, wasn't it? I blew out smoke, away from her, gentleman that I am.

She raised her eyebrows and slid onto the arm of my chair with studied ease. When she crossed her legs she let as much skin show as possible. Very nice skin, creamy and white, but hardly necessary. It wasn't like that gown was making an attempt to conceal anything.

I looked up at her the way a scientist studies a slide. "I liked you better in the dress. At least I could let my imagination do a little work."

She gestured to herself. "What's the matter with this?" Her expression was more curious than hurt.

"Nothing, but it just shows what every woman has. The equipment is pretty much the same, though I admit yours is well arranged." I shrugged and blew a smoke ring. "A guy just gets tired seeing the same show over and over again. Why don't you sit over there so we can talk?"

I pointed my Lucky at the sofa across the room.

She slipped off the arm of the chair and stood with her fists at her waist and her pretty face crinkled. "The hell with you, Mac. Who do you think you're fooling with that lousy line? It's nothing new. Your technique stinks."

"Look," I said, trying not to get sore, "I'm not pulling your own kind of hard-to-get routine, I'm being serious."

"You are, huh?"

"You brought me here to tease me and then pull the rug out from under me and give me the horse laugh. Fine. Everybody needs a hobby. But I came up here to spend a little time with a nice kid I used to know, back when your brother Billy was a pal of mine."

She sighed and I'd be lying if I said what those breasts did under the sheer nightie didn't rate a trouser salute.

But she abandoned the sex dolly persona and smirked like a real human gal and said, "Okay, okay, Mike Hammer—you win."

She moved quite naturally over to the couch, and the truth was, it was more appealing than the sashaying routine. "What the hell *did* you come up here for?"

"Anything but that. It's too early in our renewed friendship."

She smirked. "Not for some people, it wouldn't be."

"It is for me. Ready to talk a while?"

She threw her painted-toed feet up on the coffee table, then reached over to the end table and withdrew a cigarette from a silver box. I tossed her my matches and she caught them like she was playing first base, smiled her thanks, and batted her eyelashes at me.

"Stop that," I said.

"Can't blame a girl for trying."

I returned to the armchair and got on with my talk. "You ever been out to Sidon, Marion? Little tourist trap out on Long Island?"

A match stopped halfway to the cigarette and she stared at me a moment.

Then she said, "Yes. Well, not Sidon, but a place outside there. Why?"

Interesting that she'd had to think that over before answering.

"A place outside Sidon," I said. "Wouldn't be Sharron Wesley's gambling den, would it?"

"Well... actually, yes. I was there several times. It was really very nice, very pretty perched there on the ocean."

"Who took you out there?"

"A... just a fellow... Why, does it matter who?"

"It might."

"Why?"

"Sharron Wesley's been killed."

She said nothing, but her eyes were wide and the cigarette froze halfway to her lips. She was batting her eyelashes again but I didn't figure it had anything to do with trying to look sexy.

"Who took you there, Marion?"

"I'm... I'm sorry to hear that about Sharron. She could be fun."

Obviously Marion didn't want to answer my question. I tried another: "Did this... fellow of yours spend much money while you were at the casino?"

She shook her head. "On the contrary. He won about three hundred."

"That was the first time."

"What do you mean?"

"I mean, that joint wasn't as straight as Louie's. How did your 'fellow' fare after that?"

"Oh, the next time he dropped a little. Not much."

"Then?"

"I was only there with him twice, if you're trying to make the point that they suckered him up to that point. Who killed her?"

"That's what I'm trying to find out."

"Was she a friend of yours, Mike?"

"No."

"You never... made her?"

"No."

"Well, do you have a client?"

"No. Now back to *my* questions, Marion—was there much money in the joint? I mean hard cash on the tables?"

She tried to blow a smoke ring and muffed it. "Yup," she said, "enough to make our friend Louie look like a piker."

"Estimate it."

She frowned in thought, then: "Well, I watched a poker game where they used chips. The whites cost five hundred. Nobody bothered with those. The play was all with the blue. One guy had a pile as big as his belly in front of him. And he had a good-size belly."

"Any important people from the city there?"

"A few politicians. Local types. Maybe some state officials. I don't pay much attention to that kind of thing."

"What *did* you pay attention to?"

She shrugged. "Some out-of-town money from Chicago seemed to carry things that night. There were one or two society-page playboys treating some phony blondes to a showy time, too. You know, trying to impress."

"Were *you* impressed at all? I mean… what was your opinion of the place?"

"Say, you really did want to talk, didn't you?"

"I told you that."

"All right. To me it looked big-time. There was as much money there as you'll ever see out in the open, and nobody was worried about it, so the fix was in. In a town the size of that Sidon, it wouldn't be hard to do. A few hundred handed out to the bulls, and everything'd be jake."

Miss Marion Ruston really had been working for Louie Marone a while.

She went on: "It was an elegant joint, all right, with enough attractions to pull a crowd from as far away as the Midwest. I've seen some of the players in Louie's, but they weren't the *real* spenders. These playboys and rich johns, they *think* they roll high, but the boys with the *real* dough at the Wesley joint were guys who made gambling their business. I could mention a few names, but it would be better if I didn't."

"Why?"

"You may not like me, Mike. But *I* like me, Mike. I like me so much I'd hate like hell to be put on the spot."

"I like you just fine, kid. And anyway, getting put on the spot went out with Prohibition."

"Oh, did it? That's what you think! Why, only the other day I was reading a magazine article where a mobster went in for a haircut and shave and got his throat cut, instead."

I stabbed out my cigarette in a tray, and waved that off. "Nuts. Like Bugsy Siegel said, those boys only kill each other."

"You think? Didn't *he* wind up shot to hell?"

"All I mean is, they have their own fix in. As long as they pay their income tax, they have nothing to worry about. Sharron's place wasn't underground. If anybody catches hell, it'll be the operators, not the players. Giving me their names won't get them or you in any kind of hot water."

She frowned, smoking nervously now. "Are you *really* sure, Mike?"

"I'm sure."

"Well…"

She looked dubious, but decided to take the chance. "I saw Bill Evans there—from Chicago?"

"Yeah? Who else?"

"Miami Bull."

I whistled at that. Those two guys were the biggest of the big in gambling circles. When they sat in a game, it was for tens of thousands. If that was the kind of crowd that played at her "parties," Sharron Wesley had cleaned up.

"Do you know a local Sidon cop named Dekkert?"

Marion laughed gaily. "*That* big phony? Ha! Last time I was out there, he spent the whole darn night putting the make on me, or anyway trying to. Can you beat that?"

"Tell me more."

She sat forward, dishing the dirt. It's in a dame's blood. "He took me out in the back and walked me to the beach. He said he was worried about something he saw my date do, and wanted a private word. We passed a clump of bushes and he tried to throw me down to drag me in there."

"The damn rape-happy slob…"

"Oh, it was funny! I got my hands on a rock and bashed him in the puss. He went out like a light. Was *he* burned up! When he crawled back in half an hour later, he couldn't look at me the rest of the night without going red as a monkey's rear-end. And he had a mouse under his eye big enough to put in your pocket and feed cheese to."

It was pretty funny, the way she put it. Dekkert must have felt like a dope to be pushed over by a young broad like Marion. Trying to force himself on a kid, well, that was one more score to settle with the bastard.

I said, "Who was Dekkert around there? Not a customer surely."

"No! He was the bouncer at Sharron's. At least that's what he told me. He never bounced anybody that *I* saw. The out-of-town big shots, like Evans and Miami Bull, they all carried rods anyway, and I don't think Dekkert could have pushed them very far."

"How do you know they packed rods? They didn't go around with their coats off, did they?"

She grinned at me, the real girl under the sex kitten façade in full evidence now. "Listen, Mister Man, I've been around punks so long that a hood with a rod on his hip, or under his arm, couldn't hide it from me even if it were small enough to be a watch fob."

That made me laugh.

She pointed with her cigarette. "Like that rod under *your* left shoulder. It must be a big one. I always figured you for a big gun, Mike."

So we were back to that routine again. Full circle.

I stood. "Okay, thanks, Marion, you told me enough for one night. And I appreciate it. Maybe after I've dug into this thing a little deeper, I'll drop back and see you again."

She leaped to her feet, eyes flaring. "You mean you're *going?*"

"Sure. I got what I came for." I slapped my hat on and walked to the door.

She grabbed my arm and spun me around. "You can't leave yet!"

"Why?" I let my eyes laugh at her.

"You didn't even *try*. We didn't even get started. And you promised."

"I don't remember promising you anything, kiddo."

"All that talk about skipping the preliminaries! You talked real big! You—"

Before she could finish that thought, I reached up and gripped her dressing gown at the neck, then gave it a vicious yank. The light material of the wrapper ripped like paper. I tossed it away like a used tissue and had a look at my handiwork.

She stood there stark naked, her eyes glowing like hot coals, her mouth open with surprise. I looked her over coolly. She did have a lovely body.

"Nice," I admitted. "Still… nothing that unusual."

I pulled a ten spot from my pocket and stuck it in

her hand. "That's for the gown. Maybe you better get a housecoat next time. It'll save you catching a cold."

When I closed the door, a vase smacked against the wood and smashed into fragments. I usually had to know a girl a lot better before the pottery started flying. Maybe next time she wouldn't try so hard, and we really could have a little fun.

I walked to the corner intending to catch a cab back to the garage where I'd left the heap, then on impulse stopped by a drugstore and slipped into a phone booth.

After three tries I got Pat, at home this time.

"Hello, buddy. Mike again."

"Mike, I figured you'd be back in Sidon by now."

"I'm about to head that way. But some things have happened since I saw you this afternoon."

"You do lead an eventful life."

I filled him in on the two thugs who'd been rifling my office, and the ensuing scuffle.

He didn't even bother telling me I should have reported it. But he did ask, "Could you identify either of them?"

"By their clothes maybe, but the lights were out and the blinds closed. Their faces were a blur. Does this qualify as connecting the Sidon case to the city?"

He snorted a laugh. "Like there aren't three dozen hoods in this town with other reasons for shaking down your office."

"Okay, then, how about this? I have a little more information for you on the late Sharron Wesley."

"Do you now?"

"These names do anything for you? Miami Bull and Bill Evans—from Chicago? They've been sitting in out at the Wesley casino."

A long, low whistle came over the wires. "Party girl Sharron was running a pretty high-rolling operation. This is more than just rich kids and dilettantes throwing some loose change around."

"Sure as hell is. The take out there on any given weekend had to be plenty high. Look, I need to get back to Sidon. If you want me at all, call that hotel."

"Got it. Should have something for you in a day or so."

"Good. See you."

Sunday night, cabs were scarce but I finally snagged one, and had it head over to the garage near the Hackard Building to pick up my heap. The cab rolled through a nighttime city cool and calm with twinkles of light and touches of neon giving it a soothing, dreamy quality.

But I knew the statistics.

Somebody would be getting killed out there, right now.

I wanted to get back to Sidon before midnight if I could. Luckily, the roads were empty. Under a star-studded sky so clear and so deep a blue Hollywood might have had a hand in it, I stepped it up to seventy, then eighty, flying through darkness, chasing my own bright headlights.

The miles rolled by. I stopped once at a dog wagon and had a bite to eat before I went on. It was eleven-thirty when I saw Sidon up ahead, its lights reduced to a small swarm of fireflies. In less than a minute, I hit the outskirts.

I rolled the buggy into a corner of the parking lot behind the hotel and hustled into the lobby, anxious to sit down with Velda and catch each other up. From the crowd that sat around, you would think it was maybe seven at night and the town was enjoying a mid-summer boom.

One of the loungers spotted me and yelled, "*Here* he is!"

A half dozen guys came running, dragging scratch pads from their pockets. Finally the reporters had caught up to me, shouting questions.

"What have you got, Mike?"

"How about the lowdown?"

"Michael, these city hicks are clammed up tight!"

I spoke to the knot of men around me. "Nothing much, fellers. Sorry, but I haven't really gone to work yet. Still in the prelim phase."

"Cut it, Mike, it's all over town that somebody took a shot at you!"

That stopped me cold.

"Where did you get that from?" I asked them.

A little chunky guy from the *Chronicle* spoke up. "It's just a rumor around town, but I got in to see the local doctor..."

Had Doc Moody sold me out?

"...and he told me about that potshot, Mike, and I told the boys, but how the town folk found out, hell, that's no fault of mine. That good-looking secretary of yours told us to pipe down until you came back, and we did. So what's the story?"

I thought it over.

Dr. Moody had not sold me out—instead, he'd pulled a smart one. Let the reporters get an idea of what had happened and there would be no tricks played on Poochie by the local bully boys. A swell move on the doc's part, gaining my full approval after the fact.

I cooperated with the bunch of newshounds by telling them what happened.

"Mike Hammer," somebody said, laughing, "saved by a beachcomber! We should stop the presses."

Another asked, "Any idea who shot at you? Was it the same guy who murdered Sharron?"

"Well, as it happens," I said, "I *do* know who tried to gun me down."

Anyway, I figured I did, and saying this might smoke Dekkert out. He'd either make another try for me or jump down my throat. He still was the law in this town, after all. Either way, I'd have some real fun.

With their rapt attention, I continued: "It's very possible that Sharron Wesley's killer did try to take me out. Perhaps even probable. This is a small town, where there hasn't been a killing in years. How likely is it that *two* murderers would be at large?"

"So it's *one* perpetrator?"

"I'm not sure... *yet*."

I let the significance of that linger. The reporters exchanged glances.

"Can we quote you on this, Mike?"

"Sure, go ahead."

I went on and told them of Sharron Wesley's gambling set-up and the way the town was operated, without mentioning the mayor by name. They could fill that in themselves. I also omitted Poochie getting beaten by Dekkert and his goon squad. I didn't have to mention Dekkert's checkered past with the New York PD because every one of these newsmen had covered that story years ago.

What I gave them seemed to satisfy them, and they closed their pads.

A little guy from the *News* piped up: "Hey, Mike. Think there's any use us sticking around any longer?"

"Why not? Before I'm through someone's sure to get shot up."

Several of them laughed at that. Several others didn't—they knew I meant it.

"Guess you're right," the little guy said, sticking his

pad in his sportcoat pocket. "Always could depend on getting a good story out of your exploits. Can't print all the details sometimes, but every damn time a darn good story. Okay, I'm sticking. What about you guys?"

The others grinned and nodded. They were happy as long as there was a bar handy and an expense sheet to pad. If a story panned out, great. If not, so what? They still had a paid vacation far enough away from town that the city editor couldn't ride their tails.

When they drifted away, I picked up the house phone and asked for Velda's room. The operator rang a few times, but no one answered. I thanked her, hung up and took the stairs to my room. There was no note under the door for me, so I took the chance that she was off eating or still snooping around.

I laid out a suit for tomorrow and was switching my junk to the other pockets when I pulled out that feminine handkerchief from the side coat pocket. It still smelled of the musky perfume. I sniffed it and put it with the rest of my stuff. I had almost forgotten that little item.

The phone rang and it was Velda. "Mike, when did you get back?"

"Little while ago. I gave an impromptu press conference for the boys in the lobby, then tried your number but got no answer."

"I was down the hall taking a shower. Come on over."

I did, and she answered the door in a white terrycloth robe that came almost to the floor. Her hair was damp and she toweled it as she sat on the edge of the bed and I pulled up a chair so we could talk.

I filled her in on my day, and when I got to the part where I'd got into it at the office with the two intruders, she came over and checked the back of my head. She smelled great. It was just soap, but, man...

"You'll live," she said, and sat back down on the edge of her bed. "What then?"

I told her about my visit to Louie's, and decided the better part of valor would be to omit going to Marion's crib. Moving the gist of that conversation to Louie's place wouldn't hurt anything, and there was no need to get Velda's nose out of joint. The Ruston girl parading herself for me, and yours truly pretending not to be interested, would not seem the harmless fun it had been. Not to a secretary who gave me hell for two weeks after spotting one lousy lipstick smear on my shirt collar.

"So Sharron's silent partner," Velda said, "is some big gambler from the city. It wouldn't be this Miami Bull character you mentioned, or…?"

"Bill Evans. No—wrong city. They're Chicago boys."

"I hear there's crime in Chicago."

"Yeah, I heard that rumor, too, but this will be some big boy from New York, and I may try to track down Evans and Miami Bull to lead me to him. They won't have anything to lose."

"Our friend Dekkert has ties in the city."

"That fact is not lost on me, honey. How was *your* day?"

She put her hands on the terrycloth over her knees and rocked like a little girl. "Quiet. You'd almost think I was on vacation."

"Ouch."

"I had a few conversations with locals, but most of the stores weren't open. Either closed on Sunday or not open for the season yet."

"No surprise."

She went back to toweling her hair. "I spoke to several reporters, but I knew more than they did. They got wind of Doc Moody, but I handled that."

"So that was your fine hand at work? Good job all

around. What about Poochie? Did you see him today?"

She smiled tightly. There was frustration in it.

"I did," she said. "But the doc is mostly keeping him sedated. I finally spoke with the little guy this evening, but you're not going to like what I found."

"He didn't finger Dekkert as the shooter in the window?"

She shook her head. "At first he said he didn't remember. Then when I pressed, he said he just saw the gun and that a man was holding it. But it was too dark outside for him to see who was aiming the gun."

"Do you believe him?"

"I'm not sure. Maybe you can get more out of him. I pressed as hard and as long as the doctor would allow. Obviously, the poor soul may just be scared, Mike. Dekkert almost killed him the other night. And getting beaten to death is a hard way to go."

I nodded. "Say, you look tan. Don't tell me you actually got some sun?"

"I did!" She hopped off the bed. "Want to see?"

"Easy there, kitten…"

"Oh, don't be a prude. You're a big boy."

Getting bigger all the time.

"I have a bra and panties on," she said, "you coward. My bikini is skimpier, you know."

She opened the terrycloth robe. It was like curtains parting on a masterpiece of sculpture devoted to the female form. She had a nice tan going, all right, nicely dark against the underthings. And I had seen her in a two-piece suit before, but the psychology of seeing her that way, presenting herself to me with a proud smile, letting me admire the jut of her breasts, the curve of her hips, the hint of dark curls behind the whiteness of panty, the long, long legs, not the pipe cleaner legs of a model but the fully fleshed, muscular legs of a vibrant woman.

"What do you think?" she said, as she closed the robe and cinched the terrycloth belt.

"I think," I said, managing to get to my feet, "that it's been a long day, and I could use a shower myself. A cold one."

She laughed and showed me to the door.

"See you in the morning," she said.

"See you, kitten."

You're here to find a killer, buster, a voice in my head said.

"If these dames don't kill me first," I muttered.

CHAPTER EIGHT

The two naked bodies were strung by their heels from a rafter in the barn, their fingertips almost brushing the warped planked flooring. Dried blood in frightful trails from countless wounds made vertical stripes down twin flesh in horrible design. The smears of blood beneath had clotted, merging into each other like an obscene Rorschach test ink-blot pattern peppered with blow flies trying to feast there.

The dignity of death was missing. The skillful surgery that had been performed on each, slowly and intricately, had wiped all that out. It was more like taking a look inside a slaughterhouse on a hot day.

Or maybe that was just my opinion because I had seen this kind of horror before and could be almost objective about it now. Not quite, but almost. The one thing that stood out was that, at one time, those two girls had been pretty.

I handed the grisly photograph back to Dave Miles.

"I remember reading about it," I said. "Early this spring, right? But this doesn't really resemble the Sharron Wesley killing."

Dave had called me early at the Sidon Arms—seven o'clock. He had seen the write-ups in both the local and New York papers, saw my name, and called me. He said to come right out to his Quonset hut office at the brick manufacturing works near Wilcox. I pushed a note under Velda's door, grabbed a napkin-wrapped cruller and paper cup of coffee at Big Steve's, and took the heap for a thirty-mile spin.

"The common thread," Dave said, "is beautiful nude women. Dead ones."

"That's typical fare on a sex killer's menu."

"Mike, my gut tells me it's the same sick bastard. And there's *another* kill, one none of the police authorities have ever connected up."

One time Dave had been a big man, physically and professionally, an inspector in the New York PD, and Pat's immediate superior.

But even as an inspector, Dave couldn't stay off the street and two years ago he had gone in an apartment after a killer and a blast from the punk's shotgun had taken off his lower leg, and he'd had to retire. He wound up as head of security at the brick-making plant that was Wilcox's only industry besides tourism.

Now he sat behind his desk, looking slightly shrunken in an old suit, his plastic leg a disembodied thing propped against the windowsill behind him. A frown creased his face into a caricature of weariness and he shook his head.

"Oh, hell, Mike. Maybe you're right to be skeptical. I just saw the write-ups in the papers this morning, and your name in the middle of it, and…"

I jammed a butt in my face and lit up. "Okay. So what's this *other* kill?"

Some life came into his eyes and he leaned forward. "Six months ago a girl was strangled with her own nylon stocking out on a stretch of beach. Her clothes were gone. Never found. She lay there with the stocking that killed her still knotted around her throat."

"Where was this?"

"Down a side road, about halfway between here and Sidon."

He had my attention. Two strangulations. Two dead naked females, pretty ones.

"Whose case?" I asked.

"The Suffolk County Sheriff's department."

"What do you know about them?"

"They're closer to real cops than the Sidon crowd, or our bunch here in Wilcox either. But it was months ago, and they weren't able to run anything down."

"Months ago when?"

"The strangled girl was early last fall, right after the season ended. You probably remember from the papers that the girls strung up in the barn were found on the other side of Wilcox. Just outside town but within the city limits."

"Making it a Wilcox PD matter."

"Yeah. Why, is that significant?"

I shrugged, blew a smoke ring and watched it dissipate. "Maybe. If you have a sex fiend at large, you may just have a smart one. For the sake of argument, say he did kill the Wesley dame, too. That means in a fairly small area, he has managed to spread the killings out among three different jurisdictions—two small-town police forces and the sheriff's department."

"Can a maniac be that organized?"

"They never caught Jack the Ripper, did they? Look, what makes you tie it in? You're not a cop, anymore. This has nothing to do with guarding a brick-making factory on the Island."

Those hard pale blue eyes stared into my own and a grimace touched his mouth. "Because once you're a cop, Mike, you never stop. Do I have to tell *you*? And I can smell it. These murders are connected."

"Smells don't hold up in court," I said.

"But they sure can lead you to the rotten source though, can't they?"

I chuckled dryly and had another drag on the Lucky. "I came to listen, Dave, and I'm almost interested. Make it fit. I don't know the details."

"They were women, they were young, they were pretty, now they're dead. There's a sex angle to each of them."

"Sharron Wesley wasn't all that young—she was in her late thirties. And she wasn't molested." Doc Moody's autopsy had said as much.

"*None* of these victims were molested, and that's a telling link. Stripping them and killing them, that's the sex angle."

Which meant it didn't have to be a "he"—they made killers in both male and female models.

"There's one difference," I reminded him. I thumped the crime-scene photo on his desk. "These kids were tortured to death."

Dave Miles grinned at me, a hard, nasty grin. "I'm disappointed in you, Mike. Don't you see the similarity in the crime scenes?"

"Are you kidding? A barn? The beach? A body found draped on a stone horse in a park, a week after the killing? There's no similarity at all."

"Sure there is. Maybe you just haven't rubbed the sleep out of your eyes."

I had another look at the photo.

And it came to me: *the murderer had arranged each crime scene with a dramatic flair designed to turn his victims into a sort of grotesque tableau.*

"Those crime scenes," Dave said, "are staged for effect. For maximum impact. Like they were posed for a shot in a sleazy true-crime magazine."

I tossed the photo back on the desk. "Okay. You have a point. But this isn't New York, Dave. Who did the autopsies on the Wilcox barn girls?"

"We have a competent coroner in Wilcox. He says the girls were slowly slashed to death. Death by a thousand cuts. Hung up for slaughter, with their ankles bound above them and the wrists roped, and the fiend took his sweet time. The dirt floor was caked with blood an inch thick."

He was trying to get me going. Pushing every button he could. Why?

I stayed professional. "The two strangulations make a similar modus operandi, but this torture kill, it's different. You're throwing me a curve, buddy. What did the Wilcox police have to say?"

His grin seemed to tighten down. "That's the kicker, Mike. We don't really *have* any. The city force has nine men who are only employees and don't do much more than tag cars or arrest an occasional drunk. Yes, there's this factory here, but otherwise we're as much a tourist town as Sidon."

"So who makes up this lackluster force?"

"They're all local men who get hired when there's an opening, given a briefing, then issued a uniform, badge and gun and assigned a beat. Most of them are military returnees using it as a between-jobs bridge. Out here we have an elected constabulary system with three men patrolling for speeders."

Could a thrill killer have selected this little part of the world to take advantage of the kind of half-assed policing that Sidon and Wilcox had to offer? If so, that was damn shrewd—here we were, in Manhattan's backyard, but well away from the jurisdiction of the kind of trained scientific professionals represented by Captain Pat Chambers.

I muttered, "Big fish in a little pond…"

"What, Mike?"

I stabbed out the spent Lucky and got another one going. "How about the Suffolk sheriff's office?"

"That's the other kicker. Last November John Harris didn't run for re-election. He was a damn good man… made Deputy Chief Inspector in New York before he came up here, but he was diabetic and couldn't take it after two terms in office."

"Yeah, I know John. You're right. Good man."

Dave shrugged. "Maybe he could have taken care of this thing, but he died a month back."

"Hell. I hadn't heard."

"His deputy was the only other trained person around, but when Harris quit, so did the deputy—took a job someplace out west."

"So who's in now?"

"Oh, Fred Jackson, a nice enough guy, all right, real nice guy. He was elected by popular acclaim just *because* he was a real nice guy."

"Great," I said. "Just fine."

"He was born here, went to college upstate, taught six-graders for a year, got drafted and picked up some shrapnel in the Pacific, became something of a local hero and inherited his old man's dairy farm. Now he's sheriff."

"No good, huh?"

"A nice guy, but no cop, Mike. No cop at all."

"And you smell something."

"That's right. The county sheriff's office is right here in Wilcox. You could talk to Sheriff Jackson, if you think it'll do any good."

"So could you. You're still around."

"That's about the extent of it," he told me. "*Around.* Nothing more. Every so often they take off another hunk of my leg to try and stop happening whatever's happening to it. Pretty soon there won't be much left to take off. I can make it back and forth to the office, do my job well enough to hold it down, because I can still yell loud enough to scare people. And I have a few guys at the plant here back me up."

A scowl pulled at my eyes. "What do they need security for in a place that digs up clay and makes bricks out of it?"

"Because our big contract is with the government. There's a rare element in this ground that makes our bricks ideal for use in government facilities attached to atomic testing."

"So you're keeping the Commies away."

He grinned. "No Ruskies have made it past Staten Island on my watch."

I laughed at that, but I was getting itchy to get back to Sidon and my real case.

I said, "Listen, Dave, I can see why you think the Sharron Wesley killing might tie in to these others. It strikes me as kind of thin frankly, but… I can see it. What you don't know is she was likely killed because of that casino she ran outside of Sidon. She appears to have stashed substantial cash on the grounds, just begging for a treasure hunt, and she has ties to big-time gambling in the city. Unless syndicate guys have suddenly started hiring kill-happy lunatics to carry out contract work, I can't see how this ties in."

He didn't reply at once. Then he said, very softly, "You and I have been friends too damn long for you to just shrug me off, Mike. You backed me up in a shoot-out twice and I damn well saved your ass when Gorcey had a gun in your neck and was going to blow your damn head off."

There was something hanging in the air I couldn't quite make out.

Finally I said, "Okay. So I owe you. You probably owe me, too, but forget that. I know you have good instincts. Hell, great instincts. But so do I. There's more to this."

"There is."

"Then spit it out."

Dave nodded slowly, then pushed his chair around with his good leg and stared out the window at the complex of buildings that sprawled out to the west.

His voice was distant as he said, "Remember that little teenage girl whose family got killed when Thaxton burned down his building to collect the insurance?"

"Sure. She was a sweet kid. Doris something, right? Doris Wilson? You had me enlist Velda to put her up for a month before you found somebody to take her in. Nobody back in those days on the department ever knew how much of a soft-hearted slob you really are."

His head half-turned, then he looked back out the window. "Nobody else ever took her in, Mike. *I* gave her a place to stay, saw to it she stuck out school and made sure she had whatever she needed. Helen and I, we never had any kids, you know. We couldn't."

I let him talk. My gut told me where this going, though I prayed I was wrong.

"When Doris graduated, she went to business college and wound up with a job right here in Wilcox. Here at the plant."

"Damn," I said.

"We stayed close. And if your dirty mind is thinking I was anything more than a father figure to her, then screw you, Mr. Hammer. After Helen died, I never wanted another woman. Maybe I was still doing things for the kid we never had. It wasn't any trouble. More like a pleasure. Taking this job here was sort of like coming home for Doris and me, you know what I mean?"

I nodded, but he didn't see me.

"That's why I called you," he said.

I still didn't say anything. Slowly, he swung around in his chair and got another photo from his desk. Something had happened to his face—it looked gaunt and tired now. He handed me the photo.

It was another crime-scene shot, this one of the girl on the beach with the nylon stocking around her neck and her eyes popping and her tongue bulged out and her body arranged in an obscene spread-eagle that made a mockery of her beauty.

I hadn't seen her since she was a kid, but it was Doris, all right.

I stabbed my Lucky out. "It's a damn shame," I said. "But I barely knew this girl. I'm not saying this doesn't make me sick to my soul, but I'm already on that other Sidon killing."

"This is *another* Sidon killing, Mike. And I'm telling you with every fiber of cop instinct left in this fouled-up body of mine, it ties in. And you're the one to settle the score."

Softly, I said, "Me?"

Those pale blue eyes were as hard and cold as ball bearings, but with a flaming rage at their core so intense I could hardly meet them.

"You. You'll do it because we're friends. And you'll do it because you're as professional a cop as any could hope to be, but you aren't hampered by rules and regulations."

That wasn't fair—he'd heard me say that often enough and now he was feeding it back to me.

"And, Mike—you're the goddamnedest, most cold-blooded killer I have ever seen in my life. And… you're good at it."

I looked down at my hands and suddenly the weight of the .45 under my left shoulder seemed a little too heavy. When I looked up my face felt tight.

"I've had judges tell me that more than once. I can't say I liked it."

He didn't back off an inch. "Well, tough shinola, sport! Because it happens to be true. I *know* you. Any time you pull the trigger, you are in the right. The bleeding hearts will never understand people like us. So feel flattered instead of getting touchy about it. I've killed people too and never lost sleep over it."

That was more than I could say.

"Anyway," he said with an awful casualness, "you're a killer, not a murderer… and murderers *need* killing. Somebody has to do it. And I am electing you."

"If you didn't have one leg I'd knock you on your ass," I said, halfway meaning it. "Even you being an old man wouldn't bother me any."

"You're the one going soft, Mike," he said with a grin. "You should've done it already."

"Soft my ass. You pull me in here by the short hairs and expect me to like it?" I slammed a fist on the beach photo. "I was around that nice kid for a month before you got her squared away, and I can remember back. You're a bastard, Dave. Laying this crap on me."

Those pale blue eyes watched mine again and he said, "Okay. Blow the whistle and cry foul. All I ask is, play your hand out in Sidon. If it ties in, it ties in. If it doesn't, we'll talk again, and maybe get you to look into these kills. Because if somebody doesn't step in, there will be others, Mike."

He was right—whoever had been behind that torture kill in the barn was not going to stop. The hunger of whatever sick sexual satisfaction he felt in expressing his power and savagery over these innocents would want feeding again, and again…

Outside, the sun was heading higher, throwing an orange glow on the tops of the buildings, sparkling off the trees behind them. I stood up and shoved on my hat.

"Okay, Dave." I stopped halfway to the door. "But lay off on the cold-blooded killer stuff, okay?"

He leaned back in his chair and nodded solemnly. "Sure, Mike. We'll let some sick bastard find it out for himself."

Like Sidon, Wilcox counted on the tourist trade, but unlike its neighboring community, it had the look of a real, quietly prosperous town. A block of storefronts had attractive display windows with apartments above, all the buildings uniformly white brickwork with bright, shiny metal trim. And on the corner at the end of the business district was a two-story white-brick building with a fresh, post-war look and, over the entrance, big metal letters that spelled out SUFFOLK COUNTY SHERIFF'S DEPARTMENT.

I parked the heap at the curb, went in, and walked up to a counter that kept civilians away from a busy bullpen of tan-uniformed officers. Despite Dave's misgivings, this place had a professionalism that underscored the joke that the Sidon PD had become.

Behind the counter, a tall, slender but curvaceous policewoman rose from a desk to greet me. With her short dark hair and black-framed glasses, she seemed to be working at not looking attractive but not making it. Even the lack of lipstick and the disinterest in her eyes couldn't dull her appeal. There was just something about a girl in uniform...

"My name is Mike Hammer. I'm a detective from New York City. Private operator working on a case. Is Sheriff Jackson in?"

"Well, Mr. Hammer, you obviously don't have an appointment with the sheriff. I can check his book. He might be available this afternoon."

"What time do you get off for lunch?"

That flustered her. "Uh, what do you mean?"

"I mean what time do you get off for lunch. If I have to kill a few hours in your lovely burg, I might as well pass them pleasantly. A nice long lunch with you would make the time just fly. You know the town and I don't. Where shall we go?"

"Let me check with the sheriff," she said, and she didn't mean about her lunch hour. Her cheeks were flushed as she reached for the phone. Somebody needed to tell her she could be a professional without trading in her charms.

She said, "Chief, there's a Mr. Hammer from New York to see you. He's a detective working—oh... Certainly, I'll send him right in."

The fact that I was important enough to rate immediate entry to the sheriff's inner sanctum thawed out the policewoman just a little. She gave me a nice smile as she knocked on the wood-and-glass door just off the bullpen.

"Come in!" a male voice called.

She nodded and said, "Eleven."

"What?"

"I take an early lunch. Eleven."

She winked, went off, and I was thinking, *Well, I'll be damned*, and strolled on in.

The sheriff wore a business suit with a dark-blue tie, not a uniform, and might have been a banker. He had a rugged, broad-shouldered look that had probably served him well as a political candidate, though his blond hair was thin and ineffectively combed over. Better stick to local elections.

He half-rose and extended his hand. I took it and his grip was firm. His smile was as business-like as his suit as he gestured to the visitor's chair opposite his big mahogany desk.

They had some money to spend in Suffolk County, thanks to the tourist trade—this office was richly wood paneled with wooden filing cabinets, and my brogans were resting on carpet, not wood or tile. There was a big fancy county seal on the wall behind the chief, as well as some framed diplomas and photos, several of them color shots of him grinning with buddies in the Pacific. Navy guys in a tropical clime.

"I've heard of you, of course, Mr. Hammer. We do get the city papers all the way out here in the sticks."

"I wouldn't call Wilcox the sticks, Sheriff Jackson. You've got a handsome little town here. Population's around, what? Twenty-five thousand?"

"Just twenty, but it swells to fifty during the season. Your notoriety in a number of cases isn't the only reason I had no trouble recognizing your name, Mr. Hammer. Just this morning, in the press, you were mentioned in relation to the Sharron Wesley murder in Sidon."

"Yeah, I'm looking into that."

"In cooperation with the police department there?"

"What police department?"

His smile was immediate. "If I remember right, from one particular profile the *News* did of you and your colorful career, you served in the Pacific, too."

"I did."

"I'm glad that's behind us."

"Yeah. Listen, I was just talking to my friend Dave Miles out at his plant—"

"Terrific guy, Dave. How the hell is he?"

"Well, he's fine as long as he doesn't try to run a marathon. He pointed out some similarities between the murders of Doris Wilson and Sharron Wesley."

He frowned. With his high forehead, that was a lot of frown. "Boy, I've read about the Wesley thing in the papers, but I can't say I see any connection."

"I didn't say connection. I said similarity. The victims were both strangled, the bodies were unclothed, and the crime scenes were staged. As if for effect. Also, one body was on the beach and another in a park off the beach."

"Well, not the same beach."

"Not the same stretch of it, no. My understanding is you haven't turned anything up on the Wilson case."

He shook his head glumly. "Very little."

"The similarities are there. I agree they are inexact, but Dave seems to think it may be the same killer as whoever tortured and killed those girls in that barn outside town, a few months ago."

"That isn't our case. That took place within Wilcox city limits." He reached for the phone. "I can arrange for you to talk to Chief Chasen, if you like…"

"No. Not just yet, anyway. I have to say, I'm not convinced these murders are connected myself. It's even possible someone killed Sharron Wesley and tried to make it look vaguely similar to this other killing, to muddy the waters."

"That kind of thing has happened."

"But I want to be up on this case. Two strangulations, two naked female corpses, there's enough there that I want to carry any information available into my inquiry into the Wesley killing."

He had started nodding halfway through that. "I'm afraid we have very little."

"What *do* you have? Maybe if I could see the file—"

"There's really not enough to bother getting it out. Doris' car was found outside a roadhouse where she'd been seen dancing."

"Was she there with a date?"

"No. Not even a girl friend. Some of her gang from work hung out there, and it was typical of that crowd to show up alone or in pairs or even in groups. She was a little tipsy—the autopsy showed a fairly high alcohol content in her bloodstream—and left about eleven, by herself."

"This is that roadhouse between here and Sidon?"

"Right. The Hideaway. We questioned everybody there, from Doris' co-worker friends to every waitress and both bartenders. Even the darn cooks, we talked to, and they never stuck their heads out of the kitchen."

"Somebody grabbed her in that parking lot."

"That is our theory. But we checked it. I even borrowed some lab boys from New York to go over that parking lot, and you know what they came up with? Gravel."

"Anything else in that file?"

"Nothing pertinent."

"Okay." I rose and shook his hand again. I nodded toward the framed photos. "That's the Philippines, right?"

"Uh, yeah." He gave me an embarrassed grin. "We were on this island, handling supply lines. The Japs were hiding in these caves in the hills, and it got a little hairy. You know, they'd come out at night, looking for food. Grenade went off and I took some shrapnel. And you know, there were these native girls, but you could catch eight kinds of clap if you weren't careful. Where were you?"

"In a fox hole," I said, standing at his door. "Call Chief Chasen and tell him I'm stopping by, would you?"

* * *

Chief Chasen's office was spare, but then so was the chief, a lanky Ichabod Crane kind of guy in a blue uniform. He was about forty and had an Adam's apple that bobbed as he spoke and fought with his words for your attention.

"You know, there might be a tie-up at that," he said, his voice a mellow baritone that might attract the ladies if he wasn't otherwise a scarecrow. Of course, it had worked for Sinatra.

I said, "With the Wesley killing, you mean?"

"Yeah. Let me make a call." He got on his phone and asked for "the paper evidence from the March 27 killing."

Then he returned his attention to me. "The night of their murders, those two girls were seen in a bar in Sidon."

"Sidon, huh? They were of drinking age?"

"Yeah, they were college girls from the city, but they were both twenty-one. Anyway, they took a booth at this bar. They weren't with anybody, they were just laughing and talking. We questioned several local guys who went over and talked to them, just flirting, not getting anywhere. The girls said they were meeting some fellas somewhere, and that's as much as we got."

"Okay. So how did they wind up in that barn back in Wilcox?"

"Their car was found just outside Sidon. They'd had a flat. We had a witness come forward who was driving by when the two girls were getting into a fancy car."

"What kind of fancy car?"

He shrugged. "That's all the witness had to say. He just noticed these good-looking girls piling into a fancy car of some kind, leaving another vehicle along the side of the road with a flat tire."

"Which way was the 'fancy car' headed?"

"Toward Wilcox, all right."

"You checked thoroughly into the witness?"

"Yes. He had his wife with him and we talked to her, too. Nothing there. Just a good citizen coming forward… Ah, Officer Winch, let's have that evidence."

A fresh-faced young cop had come in carrying a clear evidence envelope, which he handed to the chief, who handed it to me as the young cop went out.

"Where did you find this?" I asked, looking at the clear little bag and its contents.

"In that car with the flat tire. It certainly wasn't on the victims—they were strung up naked as jaybirds in that barn, poor things. We never did find their clothes."

Her clothes were gone, Dave Miles had said of the girl left strangled to death, naked and spread-eagled on the beach. *Never found.*

Did that detail bind these killings together as surely as the nylon around Doris Wilson's pale young throat?

I pondered that as I sat there staring at the contents of the clear evidence envelope: a matchbook with a festive New Year's motif emblazoned with the words SIDON ARMS COCKTAIL LOUNGE.

By late morning I was back in Sidon, sitting in a booth across from Velda in the hotel bar where that matchbook had come from.

"I'm starting to think Dave is right," I said. "Maybe these killings *are* the work of one maniac on the loose."

A goddess in a yellow blouse, Velda gestured with both hands, palms up. "But how does a maniac fit in with Sharron Wesley's gambling house? Not to mention all the dirty dealings our friend Dekkert is neck high in."

"I don't know," I said glumly. "And anyway, I'm not convinced the kill-crazy son of a bitch who tortured and killed those college girls is behind the Wesley dame's exit. But that nylon stocking strangulation? That's close enough to Godiva to get my attention."

She shuddered. "Mine, too."

I threw down what was left of my highball. "It *feels* like I was already on the right track, looking for her silent partner in that casino. When there's a murder, nine times out of ten, the motive is money."

"But then there's that *other* one out of ten, Mike." She shook her head and the dark hair shimmered. "I admit I'm confused."

"You're not alone."

"Makes me sick to think that nice Wilson girl wound up like that…"

"Dave's right about one thing. That's a score worth settling."

She leaned across. "Listen, I almost forgot to mention— Pat called while you were out. He didn't leave any real message, of course, after you warned him not to. You want to use the pay-phone booth?"

"No," I said. "I have to kick this thing into gear. I have a few things for you to do, honey, while I'm gone."

"Gone? Again?"

"Yeah. Talk to the bartender here about those two college girls, and if he isn't the one who was on duty, find out who, and track him down."

I dug in my pocket for my roll of bills and peeled off five tens like a poker hand and passed them across to her.

I went on: "There's one taxi in this town. Round it up and head out to that roadhouse tonight, the Hideaway— put some nickels in the jukebox, be available for a dance, let a local yokel or two buy you a beer. Talk to the bartenders out there, too. Somebody may have seen something the night Doris Wilson disappeared. It's not that I don't trust these Long Island coppers to do their job, but… I don't trust 'em to do their job."

She smirked at me. "You sure know how to show a girl a good time on a vacation. Have her dance and drink with other men."

"Vacation time is over. No more vacation till we've wrapped this up. And just in case there *is* a psychopath on the loose, you keep your wits sharp and your .32 ready."

"Roger. And you?"

"I have to head back into the city. I'll talk to Pat, and by hook or by crook, I'm going to find out who Sharron Wesley was in business with."

CHAPTER NINE

I called Pat before leaving Sidon, to warn him I was on my way, and he suggested we meet at Mooney's for mid-afternoon coffee and Danish. He didn't say so, but maybe I was becoming too much of a fixture around that station house for the reputation of a captain who hoped to be an inspector some day.

I settled for a parking place two blocks from the beanery. The afternoon was sunny but cool, nice enough to make a guy wonder why he bothered going out on the Island for a getaway. Then I heard a cabbie leaning out his window to add some profane lyrics to the song his honking horn was playing, and remembered.

Pat was already in back at our usual table when I strolled in. He saluted me with the oversize mug that was a trademark of the place, in case I hadn't noticed him. I stopped a waiter and told him to bring me my own coffee and Danish, then plopped down across from Pat. With no preliminaries beyond "Hi," I began filling him in on my visit to Wilcox, from Dave Miles to the Suffolk County Sheriff to Chief Chasen.

"I have to say I'm of two minds about these killings," he said, nibbling idly at his pastry throughout our grisly conversation. "There's enough criminal activity surrounding Sharron Wesley to make it awfully damn coincidental that some maniac would just happen to single her out."

"My thinking exactly."

"On the other hand, you pick up coincidences like blue serge picks up lint. Every time I hear a cop say he doesn't believe in coincidence, I tell him to hang around with Mike Hammer for a while."

I stirred sugar into my coffee. "But are there enough similarities to put all four kills at the feet of one fiend? We have the nudity thread, but Sharron Wesley could have lost her clothes in the drink. And as for her being artistically displayed in that park, on that stone horse, well… we don't know that it was her killer who did that. That could have been some nut with a sick sense of humor."

"Yeah, the Lady Godiva angle." He shrugged. "Can't rule that out. And even where the M.O. is similar, it's different enough to be a head-scratcher."

"Be specific."

"Well, the strangulations, for example. They're not the same—you have a nylon stocking for the Wilson girl, and powerful hands for Sharron Wesley. Then you have those two coeds in that barn who got slashed up like some demented sacrifice to the Gods."

He could chow down on that Danish all he liked. I had lost my damn appetite.

"However," he said, between nibbles, "don't downplay the nudity aspect."

"How's that?"

"Well, I should say, the lack of clothes. The missing clothes."

"Not following you, buddy."

The gray-blue eyes narrowed. "There are two breeds of mass murderer, Mike. There's your quiet everyday good citizen who snaps. Who's out mowing the lawn one lovely morning, then suddenly goes inside, finds the German Luger he brought home from the war, and saunters around the neighborhood killing everybody he comes in contact with... *Bang*, there goes his next-door neighbor, *pow*, there goes the paper boy, *bing*, the mailman, *wham*, that annoying little old lady who never cuts *her* grass, and then back home and inside, *bang*, *bang*, *bang*, there go the wife and kiddies, and if the cops don't kill him before he's done, he turns the weapon on himself. That's one kind."

"And the other is the Jack the Ripper breed."

"Right. What the textbooks called a serial mass murderer. A ruthless psychopath who blends into his surroundings like a chameleon—he may be a scout master or a grocer or even a preacher. But he's slowly building a body count. The kind of guy whose backyard turns up an interesting crop, if you go digging."

"Well, I appreciate the lecture, pal, but tell me something I don't know."

He pointed at me with the remaining third of his pastry. "How about this, Mike? A serial mass murderer likes to take trophies. The Ripper took female innards." He raised an eyebrow to make his point, then interrupted himself with another bite of Danish, which he chewed as he said, "The missing clothes may be a trophy this killer collects."

"A trophy?"

"A souvenir. Something he can take out and look at and re-live a memorable experience."

"Find the clothes and I find the killer?"

"I don't guarantee it, but keep that in mind."

Something was nibbling at my mind the way Pat was at that pastry. "You said a serial mass murderer can be somebody that fits into a community, scout master, preacher. Could it be a woman?"

"Not impossible. But I've read book after book on this subject, Mike, and there just aren't a lot of female mass murderers of either stripe."

"Okay. But what about a police officer?"

"Well, sure. What better place to hide than behind a badge? It works for bent cops. It could work for a psychopathic one just as well. And a cop is somebody to whom violence is anything but foreign."

"Maybe that's how this ties up."

"What do you mean, Mike?"

"I mean our pal Dekkert. We know he's a sadistic son of a bitch. He's got a badge and can go anywhere in or around Sidon with goddamn impunity."

Pat was squinting at that, shaking his head. "Well, I don't know. Dekkert's time on the New York PD was all about money. Graft. And he had a reputation as a big, good-looking mug who never had trouble attracting the ladies."

"Maybe so, but you remember Billy Ruston's sister, Marion?"

"Sure. Cute kid."

"Cuter than that. She's all grown up and in all the right places. I ran into her at Louie Marone's last night, and she told me about a couple trips she made out to Sharron Wesley's gambling den."

He shrugged his eyebrows. "No kidding. I didn't know she was old enough to vote."

"She's old enough to do a lot of things. Anyway, seems Dekkert put the make on her, and I don't mean brought her flowers and candy. He dragged her off into the bushes and if she hadn't kneed him where babies begin, the bastard might well have raped her."

He gave me a skeptical smirk. "I suppose anything is possible. But trying to force yourself on some dolly you bought drinks for at a casino isn't the same as stringing up coeds by their ankles in a barn."

"No. No, it isn't."

"And anyway, Mike, there's no sexual assault in any of the four murders. This particular serial mass murderer may not be capable of normal sexual activity."

"Not even an abnormal activity like rape?"

"Not even that. He probably gets his sexual charge out of the violence he takes out on these girls. Those trophies he takes, he may use them in pleasuring himself."

"Sick bastard. This just keeps getting nastier and nastier." I sighed and slugged down some coffee. "Cripes. Maybe I'm trying too hard."

"Too hard to what?"

"To connect these murders up. Pat, I don't know whether I'm getting closer, or if what Dave Miles told me is a distraction—throwing me off."

Pat leaned forward, so close I could have brushed the crumbs off his mouth. But I didn't.

"Look," Pat said, "I may be able to help you out on this thing, this serial mass murder aspect, I mean… even without a direct New York City tie-in."

"That would be swell, Pat. What do you have in mind?"

He sipped coffee and gave up a tiny shrug. "I've got a friend with the state police, a Sergeant Price. I'll fill him in about these murders, and suggest that he may have a killer in his jurisdiction who may be trying to fall between the cracks by spreading his nasty games among various small-town, small-time law enforcement agencies."

"You mean, you may be able to convince Price this is a state-wide matter?"

"Yeah. Sometimes a task force can be mounted, joining elements of the involved departments, with state cops overseeing and directing. And they are *real* cops, Mike. Anyway, I can give it a shot."

"Man, that would be terrific. That keeps me from getting sidetracked."

"You mean, from looking for Sharron Wesley's silent partner?"

I nodded, and dunked my Danish. I was getting my appetite back.

Pat was smiling. "Mike, I may have something for you on that score, too. According to my informants, both Bill Evans and Miami Bull are still in town."

"Damn! That's great. Where?"

"That I don't know. Word is, there's a big poker game going on, very high stakes, into its third day. They take an hour break every five hours to rest, eat, and hit the head. Then back at it."

"Three days. May be winding down."

"May be. I'd get right on this. If I hear something else, where can I get a hold of you?"

I gobbled the rest of the Danish, threw the coffee down, and got to my feet. "I'm heading to Louie Marone's joint. After that, I have no idea. Can you catch the check? Next time'll be my turn."

"Sure," he said wryly. "Like the last three times. Shoo, fly, shoo. My God, you go out to Long Island on vacation and I see more of you around town than I have for the last six months…"

But I was halfway to the door already. I looked back, tossed him a grin and a little salute, and he just shook his head and took one last bite of Danish.

* * *

Louie was having a chat with his bartender when I came in. Business was so so, but the real business here was the gambling upstairs, and this was late afternoon. Too early for that kind of action.

Today the big genial Italian in the ancient tux didn't seem his usual happy self. He was damn near glum as he guided me to one end of the bar and we sat on two stools like any other patrons.

"I am a glad to see you, Mike."

"Yeah, I'm glad to see you, too, Louie. Always."

He frowned, almost as if he were suffering. "What *happen* between you and little Marion the other night? No, no, I don't mean to pry a into your business, Mike. But she is a nice girl, and she seems so sad today. What's it they say? Out of sorts."

I waved that off. "I just taught her that some men are immune to her charms. She better get used to it. She was bound to run into a grown-up sooner or later."

"She's a nice girl, Mike. She's a nice to have around."

"You got a crush on her yourself, Louie?"

That big mustached pan of his blushed like a school girl. "Mike… I'm a old enough to be her papa."

"Yeah, but you're not her papa. If she's such a nice girl, why let her hang here like a glorified B-girl? She's gonna get herself raped one of these days. Then see how 'out of sorts' she is."

He shrugged elaborately. "What can I do? She's my bookkeeper!"

"Not in the kind of dress I saw her in last night. She'd bust a seam taking a ledger down off a shelf. Look, I know that kid makes nice window dressing for you around this joint. But if you really value her, get her an eyeshade and some nice gray mannish business suit, have her pin her hair back, and stick her in a back room with a pencil."

He shrugged. "You probably right, Mike. I don't have a no crush on her, you unnerstan'. But I sure do like to look at her."

"Looking's free, Louie. That's one of the great things about America. You have a chance to make a few phone calls for me?"

He nodded. "I did. Found some things out, like you ask. I write down some more names. Let me go get 'em for you."

"Thanks, Lou… Bartender! Highball."

The drink had barely come when Louie trundled back. He looked upset.

"Oh, Mike, she's in a the back room."

"Marion?"

He nodded. "She's in a bad way, Mike. I tell her you was here and she say she wanna come out and talk to you, but… she start crying, and she can hardly stand up, she's so upset."

I gave him a disgusted look. "Upset or drunk?"

"Well, uh… both, Mike. She's been hitting my private stock. She keep it up, she gonna kill herself."

I grunted. "Oh, hell. You got those names for me?"

He did, written on a small sheet in a cramped hand, half a dozen names, numbers and addresses of high-rolling gamblers in the city who were likely frequenters of Sharron Wesley's casino on the Island. I recognized four of them. Some damn good leads to track down.

But I said, "Look, there's supposed to be a big high-stakes poker game going on somewhere in town. Probably at some hotel. I'm looking for Bill Evans and Miami Bull, and they're supposed to be in it."

His eyes opened wide and he nodded. "I hear about that game. Two guys in here late last night, after you was here? They were early drop-outs in that game. Too much action, they say. Thousands on every hand, Mike. Crazy how much."

"You're just jealous, Louie. So where's the game?"

"They don't mention that."

"Can you find out?"

He cocked his head and gave me a look. "Can you drive a my Marion home? I don't want her round here like this, Mike. Beautiful girl like that, with a snootful? Not so beautiful."

I tapped him on the chest with a forefinger. "I'll drive her home. You find that hotel for me."

A grin blossomed under the skinny mustache in the fat face. "It's a deal, Mike. I'll call a you at Marion's apartment."

"No, I won't be there that long. I'll stop back."

We left the bar and went through the archway where in Louie's private den sat Marion, curled up in one of the tufted leather chairs with her skirt hiked up and showing a lot of leg. Not that the tight-fitting blue-silk jersey hid much more of her than, say, a coat of paint would.

I gave her shoulder a gentle shove.

She looked up at me with half-lidded dark-blue eyes. Her slack mouth became a smile and white teeth flashed, but the eyes stayed at half-mast and I could smell the Scotch on her without even leaning in.

"Mike! You came back. Louie said… *said* you came back…"

"Yeah, I came back. Let's get you home."

"Why?" she slurred. And that word was not easily slurred. "Is it late already?"

"Late enough. Can you put on your shoes?"

"No." She gave me a bleary-eyed smile and nodded toward the heels on the floor near the chair. "Make me Cinderella. I wanna be Cinderella."

I knelt like a damn prince and eased her little feet into the little dark-blue shoes, and holding onto a slender ankle and maybe a shapely calf wasn't the worst thing that ever happened to me. I am human. And male.

But she was soused, and even in a great-looking dame, that's about as appealing as a Bowery bum's breath.

So I got her to her feet and hauled her out of there. She was wobbly on those heels, and she made little squeals of protest now and then, but she came along for the ride. Making it up that gangplank of Louie's was no picnic, but we got to the dry land of the sidewalk without either of us becoming a casualty.

The heap was parked right out front, and I loaded her in. She got settled into the passenger seat, curling up like a baby waiting to be born. She did not say a word on the ride to that renovated apartment house she lived in. She even snored a little.

Dusk had fallen and traffic lights and neons made soothing glows in the coming night, but I was too irritated to appreciate it. I had things to do. Escorting home a drunken little frill was not on my dance card.

But what the hell, Louie needed time to track down Bill Evans and Miami Bull, so I could stand to play chivalrous knight for a half hour or so. But when I walked her up the brownstone steps, an arm around her waist, those curves of hers, drunken or not, were brushing up against me in distracting ways. If chivalry wasn't dead, neither was my libido.

I got her into her flower-chintz-strewn living room and asked her, "Can you stand, honey?"

"Sure I can stand. What am I, a cripple?"

I let go of her and she collapsed in a pile on the carpet.

"What you need," I said, "is a nice cold shower."

I got her around the waist again and practically dragged her into the bathroom. She did not protest. I wasn't sure she was even conscious. There was no shower, though, just a tub. I sat her on the john and backed away cautiously, making sure she was perched there properly.

When she didn't fall off on her keister, I turned on the water and made sure it got running nice and cold. Then I played prince again, taking off her shoes.

"Stand up," I said, tossing the heels aside.

"Huh?" The half-lidded eyes didn't seem to recognize me.

"Stand up, Marion. Gotta get that dress off you."

She got to her feet, unsteady but she did it.

"Put your hands up," I told her.

"Why? Is this a stick up?" It sounded like "schtick up," which would have made me laugh if I was in a better mood. She pointed a finger at me and made shooting sounds like a kid playing cowboys and Indians.

"Marion," I said scoldingly.

She pouted and put her hands up.

I tugged the dress up over her head. Beneath she wore only flimsy step-ins and an equally flimsy bra that gave her full, pert breasts no help. Not that they needed any.

She almost fell down, getting out of the step-ins. My face was in just the right position to collect evidence proving she was a real blonde. With a put-upon sigh, I got back up and reached around her to undo the bra. She stood there, a tipsy Venus, then the sound of rushing water turned me quickly to catch the bath just before it overflowed.

That was when she shoved me in.

I went in face first and was flopping around like a flounder on deck, but I had what the flounder wanted—

all the water in the world, and when I got myself turned around, I was sitting in the tub with legs hanging over the side, my socks sopped in my soaked shoes, and the naked wench was leaning over with her hands on her knees and her breasts hanging like ripe fruit waiting to be plucked while she laughed and laughed and laughed.

"Now we're *even*, sucker!" she said.

She wasn't drunk at all!

I came clambering out of that tub after her and she yiped and then screeched a laugh, and then went running bare-ass back into the living room laughing and screaming and laughing, and I tackled her and we landed on the couch in a damp tangle.

"You little vixen," I growled.

She was laughing her head off, laughing till she was crying. "You better get out of those wet clothes, mister! You'll catch your death of cold."

I got out of those clothes all right.

The lights stayed on and I was just this big damp cold creature getting warmed by the flame of her, her mouth hungry on mine, her tongue searching, flesh quivering under my hands, full and ripe and demanding. She was no virgin nor was she terribly experienced, though she did just fine, undulating, surging, our breathing building into a shout from me and a scream from her.

"Oh Mike," she breathed. Her eyes were rolled back. "Mike... I'm drunk now... I'm drunk now, all right..."

We were under the covers in her bedroom. We were both naked. We had finished round one in the living room in a hurry. Round two had taken its own sweet time, and we were both tired and, speaking for myself anyway, very satisfied. Even if two hours *had* gone by with no detecting whatsoever, other than me finding out she was a natural blonde.

"Honey," I said, "when you were out at that casino near Sidon—"

"Not *that* again," she said, stealing the smoke, taking a drag on it, handing it back.

"Yes that. That's the case I'm on. She's dead, remember? Murdered. You mentioned that local deputy, Dekkert, getting fresh with you out there. You gave him the brush by way of a knee."

"Sure. What of it?"

"Was he just getting fresh? Or do you think you were in danger?"

"Would he have forced himself on me? Maybe. But I just think he was a big damn lug who thought he was God's gift. I can handle myself. Nobody gets in my pants without permission."

"I don't remember getting permission."

Her smile was devilish. "It was implied."

"See, that's the problem. Is Dekkert a guy who was reading the signals wrong? Or is he a rape-happy slob?"

"Either way," she said, stealing my smoke again, "I'll just bet he had to go home and put an ice pack on his balls."

That made me laugh, and she laughed, too.

"You minx—faking me out like that," I said to her, and kissed her for a while.

Then we settled back again and I lighted up a fresh Lucky and asked, "Did you ever notice Dekkert hanging around Sharron Wesley?"

"Well, he was her bouncer. So I saw them talking now and then. You know, over to the side of the big casino room. Mike, I was only out there two or three times, remember."

"Think. Anything odd. Anything that wasn't employer/employee."

She was frowning as she mulled it. She stole the cigarette back, dragged on it, stuck it back in my mouth.

"You know," she said, her expression distant as she recalled, "there was this one time, this one thing… I was walking outside with the guy I went out there with. That was the best thing about Sharron's set-up, that lovely view of the ocean. Over to one side, there are these trees… that form a kind of protective wall from any neighbors in that direction. You've been out there, right?"

"Yeah, I know what you're talking about."

"Well, there's a funny little house. A lot of trellis-type stuff, latticework with ivy, unsubstantial looking."

"A gazebo."

"I guess that's what it's called. Anyway, it's mostly just a roof over a little padded bench. Kind of a romantic-looking thing. Lovey dovey, sort of. And I was walking hand-in-hand with my date… jealous yet, Mike?"

"Boiling. Go on."

"Well, I noticed Dekkert sitting out there with her. With Sharron. They were having a conversation. It was very serious. Serious how, I couldn't say. But he might… I can't be sure, Mike, but he might have been holding her hand."

"*Not* employer/employee stuff."

"No. Not hardly. But listen, I didn't see him kiss her or anything. And he sure didn't pull her into the bushes."

"Maybe you taught him a lesson that other time."

"Maybe. I've been known to teach men lessons."

"Yeah. I had one of those earlier."

"Was it so bad?"

"Terrible. Humiliating. I really should spank you."

"Promise?"

The phone rang on her nightstand and she gave it a crinkle-nosed frown.

"Forget it," she said. "I'm busy. I don't want to be reached."

"No! Get that. It might be Louie."

She gave me a dirty look, but got it and it was Louie, all right.

"Mike," Louie said, "that poker game, it's a still goin'. It's at the Waldorf-Astoria. Pretty fancy, huh?"

"You got a room number for me, Louie?"

"I sure do," he said, and gave it to me.

"And are Bill Evans and Miami Bull still in the game?" I asked.

"They sure are," he said.

Round three would have to wait.

CHAPTER TEN

Thanks to Marion Ruston's hijinx, my suit was still damp as a dishrag. That meant a stopover at the cave in that modern cliff on the East Side that I called home. My best suit waited in the closet, tweeds custom-made to conceal my shoulder-slung .45, and perfect for where I'd be heading next—you can't walk into the Waldorf-Astoria like so much riff-raff.

But this was turning into a long day, and that cute little twist had tired me out. A hot and cold shower gave me a new lease on life, and I climbed into the dry threads feeling refreshed. Before I slipped the rod into its leather womb, I took time to shoot a few drops of oil in the slide mechanism, checked the clip, grabbed an extra one for my side suit coat pocket, then wiped down the weapon and tucked it under my arm.

I felt right at home moving through the mosaic-floored, marble-columned Waldorf-Astoria lobby. I might have been some swell dropping by the Wedgewood

Room or a business executive from Philly on his way to an important conference. Instead I was a private eye looking for a poker game.

Maybe the Waldorf seems an unlikely place for such a low-brow, illegal activity. But the kind of high stakes game involved made the setting just right. I wandered around overstuffed chairs and potted plants till I detected the bank of elevators. I told the attendant where I wanted to go and he took me there, halfway up the hotel's fifty floors.

Nobody was outside Suite 2525, no watchdogs in or out of coats cut for underarm armory. I didn't knock— bad form. This was the kind of hotel suite where you rang the bell.

The lug who cracked the door had confidence—he wasn't bothering with a night-latch. I didn't know this character but he was bigger than me, and I'm big enough. The half a bashed nose and single cauliflower ear showing said he was an ex-pug, though not on any circuit around this part of the universe.

"It's closed," the doorman rumbled.

Whether that meant the table was not open to the uninvited or that the tourney was at a late stage where additional players were not welcome, I had no clue.

I said, "I need a word with Bill Evans and Miami Bull."

"Both of them?"

"Well, one of them anyway."

"They're busy."

I flashed the badge that comes with a New York State investigator's license. Do it fast enough, it can fool people.

Not the ex-pug. "That's a private badge, bud. Shove off."

He started to close the door but I gave it the kind of straight-arm a lineman gives a blitzing linebacker, and it opened, all right, the slapping hand of it sending the gatekeeper stumbling backward.

I shut the door quietly behind me and had a good look at what I was dealing with.

He was even burlier when you saw all of him, and both ears were cauliflower. He was well-groomed for a thug, clean-shaven and in a suit almost as nice as my tweeds. But he was still just a thug, with a punch-drunk patina and no discernible weapon, and when he started at me with both fists ready, I took out the .45 the way I would a match to light a cigarette, and let him look down the barrel.

There was nothing down that dark hole that you could call comforting.

"See, I did have an invitation," I said.

He started to say something, and I thought maybe he was going to yell a warning. He probably figured this was a robbery, and that made sense because there would be plenty of cash on hand. If not on the table, near it, where the dealer played banker with the chips.

But I clamped my hand over his mouth and shoved the .45 snout in his belly and shook my head sternly, like a father to a misbehaving child.

Quietly I said, "It's not a heist, friend. I really am here just to talk to Bill Evans or maybe Miami Bull, between hands. This is a friendly call… so far."

We were in an entryway and beyond us was a marble-floored, white-throw-carpeted living room where two decorative dames sat on opposing couches over by a fireplace that this time of year was also strictly decorative. One doll was a bright-eyed blonde chewing gum and filing her nails, the other a redhead reading a fashion magazine. The redhead had her back to me and might have been naked, since all I could see was the well-coifed shoulder-length hair and bare freckled shoulders. The blonde had on a white halter top with matching bolero pants and little white heels, a creamy little cutie. Neither had picked up on the little melodrama at the entryway.

The poker game would be to the left of this tableau, in the dining room. I'd been in Waldorf suites before and the layout was always the same.

The ex-pug in the nice suit was backing up slow, his sausage-fingered mitts raised about chest high. I was pressing forward with the .45 in my right hand and the forefinger of my left hand raised to my lips, shushing him. We were pretty deep into the living room before the two dames noticed us.

The blonde yiped like a puppy with its tail stepped on and I gave her a nasty glance that shut her up. The redhead, who had green eyes and a dress and heels to match, did not seem impressed. She barely looked up from her *Vogue*.

I motioned with a finger twirl for the ex-pug to turn around and he did. With my gun in his back, I walked him through the open archway into the dining room, which had been converted for poker play. Somehow the standard multi-leaf dining room table had gone away and a big, round, green-felt table with compartments for poker chips and drinks had taken its place.

The men around the table under the cut-glass chandelier had the look of expectant fathers in a waiting room when everybody's wife was in her thirty-second hour of labor. There were six of them, serious-faced men with loosened ties and suspenders and faces that hadn't been shaved lately. On the periphery several other bodyguard types sat, reacting to our entry with professional alarm but knowing enough to keep their butts planted. Another doll—nice-looking, in a French maid get-up—was there to provide drinks when asked. From the way she slumped in her chair, next to a buffet with a silver tray on it, she hadn't been asked for a while.

The ex-pug and I just stood there till they finished the hand. I was behind him, so nobody knew about the .45 except the poor bastard with its nose nudging his back, but I couldn't see being impolite. No cash was on the table, though the pot was a couple shovelfuls of a pile of mostly blue chips.

I only made three of the faces, but one belonged to Bill Evans. Sitting across from him was Miami Bull, who I only knew by reputation, though I was confident that was him. The big slump-shouldered guy's wide beezer and his massive neck explained his nickname, though he was pale enough to have never set foot in Miami.

Evans won the big pot with three tens. Nobody made a comment as he hauled the chips in with two hands. I doubted much talking had gone on for some time now.

The ex-pug cleared his throat and finally everybody noticed us. They weren't any more impressed than the redhead. Of course, they couldn't see the gun.

"This guy wants to talk to Mr. Evans or maybe Mr. Peters."

Mr. Peters was Miami Bull.

"We're not on a break," the dealer said. He was a small mustached man who talked tough but looked like he'd break like a matchstick.

I edged out a little from behind the pug, still keeping the rod concealed. "Hiya, Bill. Been a while."

Evans broke focus enough to smile a little. "Well, hi Mike." He was stacking the chips he'd just won. That would take a while. "Guys, this is Mike Hammer. He's that crazy private eye that makes the papers all the time."

I touched the tip of my hat with my left hand. My right

still had the .45 in the ex-pug's spine, which remained our little secret.

"I just need a couple of minutes with Bill," I said. "And maybe Miami Bull." To the latter, I added: "Excuse the informality. I know we've never met."

Miami Bull replied in a nasal drone, "I ain't much on formalities," and scooted his chair back and stood. He stretched and buttons almost popped on a protuberant belly. "I could use a piss, anyhow. I'll catch you on the way back, Mike."

Everybody took that opportunity to do their own stretching, and several followed Miami Bull into the kitchen, which apparently provided passage to the nearest john.

I patted the doorman on the shoulder and said, "You can go now," and he scooted, fast enough for most of the players to notice me shoving the .45 back under my arm. No reaction from this bunch, just the poker faces you'd expect.

Bill walked over, working his neck, popping vertebrae. "I wish you'd gone into chiropractic and not policing, Mike. What can I do for you? You got more than one favor coming, after that night in Chicago you ran those Outfit wops off my tail."

"I don't need a favor, Bill. Just a word."

"Lead the way."

We left the dining room and went through the living room out onto the terrace with its view on the black-and-white checkerboard skyline where the Empire State Building hogged attention.

Bill was one of those medium guys—medium build, medium height, medium weight, with the kind of face they build crowds out of. But after hour upon hour of poker, he was way past medium into well-done—his eyes bloodshot, his stubble making his face look dirty, and his dark blond hair as greasy as bacon at a one-arm joint.

"You're a mess, pal," I said.

"No I'm not," he said with a sly half grin. "I'm winning. Glad to have an excuse to slow things down. I want this game over with so I can gather my loot and get on with my life."

"On to the next game, you mean."

He shrugged, grinned bigger. "You live the life you choose, right, Mike?"

"Right. And I sure picked a doozy, huh? Have you heard about the Sharron Wesley killing?"

He had. He knew all about her gambling set-up, too, and had been out there several times. The stakes were high. Oh, there were smaller-stakes attractions for the suckers, from slots to faro. But the poker tables were for serious play.

I said, "Sharron Wesley was no Vassar girl. She was no dope, either, but we're still talking a chorus-gal cupcake who parlayed a nice build into a rich husband."

Bill smirked. "A rich husband they say she bumped."

"I'll lay odds that's more than a rumor. But my point is, there is no way in hell that ocean-side casino was her private operation. She *had* to have a silent partner."

He nodded. "You bet she did. Is that what you're trying to find out? Don't the cops know?"

"My in is with Captain Chambers of Homicide. I don't know the vice boys that well."

"Well, if you had a contact there, maybe you wouldn't have to go around breaking up friendly card games slinging around Old Ironsides there." He nodded to where I'd stowed the rod.

"I'll keep that in mind. So illuminate me."

"There are only a handful of really big-ticket gambling

czars in this town. There's a guy who is probably not number one, but he's in the top three and he's moving up. Expanding out of the city onto the Island is part of that move. Ever hear of Johnny C?"

"Johnny Casanova?"

"That's the one."

His name was actually Casanove, but he was a pretty boy who attracted dames like flies to sugar, and the lover-man nickname had been around as long as he'd been on the scene.

"This game here?" Bill said, with a head bob back toward the dining room. "This is Johnny C's action. He was around the first few hours the first day, pressing the flesh, then made himself scarce. He doesn't gamble himself. He's too smart for that."

"That was *his* casino, outside Sidon?"

"Yes it was."

"But the Wesley dame inherited big dough. Why would she let a syndicate type like Casanova take over her private mansion, and keep her on to play hostess?"

Bill shrugged. "Word is Johnny C had something on her. Maybe proof she bumped off her rich hubby. Who knows?"

"Could she have been Casanova's mistress? If she was gone on the guy, she might hand him the keys to that mansion."

"I can't answer that. But I've sat in a couple of games in the last six months or so where Sharron Wesley was hanging around. She'd show all dolled up, and seem like she was part of the entertainment committee..." He jerked a thumb toward the blonde and redhead sitting in the living room nearby. "...but those two in there? Anybody at the table who wants to grab one by the arm, on a break, is free to do so."

"Free to do what?"

"What I said! Grab her by the arm. Haul her in that bedroom. But not Sharron. She sat around looking pretty, flirted with players, held onto their arms, cheered winners on, that sort of thing. But she never went off into the bedroom with anybody but Johnny C. And then not for long."

"Not long enough to… entertain?"

"Not unless the Great Casanova is a thirty-second man. But because she seemed, in some way anyway, to be Johnny C's moll, nobody tried anything with her, beyond just friendly flirting. Don't you get it yet? How about this, Mike? She always came with a purse. A great big purse. And I don't think it had her knitting in it."

Miami Bull came out and joined us, smoking a stogie that could use the outdoors.

Bill nodded toward me. "I was just catching up Mike here on the Johnny C and Sharron Wesley 'romance.'"

"Romance my Hungarian balls," Miami Bull droned, leaking blue smoke. "She was his damn bag man! Good-looking one, maybe, but a bag man all the way. Regular Virginia Hill."

Pat had told me about Sharron Wesley's New York visits, and her party-girl hanging-on at poker fetes like this. I should have put it together sooner. But at least I knew now.

"Gents," I said, with a hand on either of their shoulders, "you have done me a big favor. Much appreciated, and I wish you both many happy hands and one whopping pot after another."

Miami Bull grunted a laugh and waved his stogie like a magic wand. "Bill here is making hash out of both of them notions."

Bill chortled and said, "Ask him, Mike, how much he took off *me* last month?"

I was halfway into the living room when I looked back and asked, "Either of you fellas have any idea where Johnny C might hang out on a Monday night?"

"Almost *any* night," Bill said, "you can find him at El Borracho, Nicky Q's fancy bistro. Johnny's got a back booth that's as close as he comes to an office."

"Thank you, fellers."

On the way out, I stuffed a sawbuck in the breast pocket of the ex-pug doorman's spiffy suit.

I was gone before he could figure out whether ten bucks was worth what I put him through.

Nicky Q—short for some convoluted Sicilian moniker I won't even attempt—was a genial oddball whose East Side wine-and-dinery on 55th attracted café society, theatrical types, and your better class of criminal. The walls were adorned with whiskey bottle labels, losing $100 horse-race tickets, and note cards with lipstick kisses courtesy of female patrons.

El Borracho meant drunkard in Spanish, but no tamales were on the menu, though Nicky's joke two-headed "Siamese fish" was listed at four grand a serving. If you wanted Nicky to have his pet talking Mynah bird taken off its bar-side perch for frying, that would be six grand. So far no takers on either. You could get a veal cutlet, though, for only ten times what Big Steve would charge you for one back in Sidon.

I got myself a rye and soda at the bar and made my way to Johnny C's office—a corner booth near the riser-type stage, just off a dance floor actually roomy enough for dancing. But the Latin-styled orchestra was on break.

That meant Johnny C would not be out doing his Valentino routine with one of the baby dolls who sat on either side of him. A redhead and a blonde again, wearing green and white plunging gowns respectively, maybe sent from the same call service as the two at the Waldorf suite. This time it was the blonde who seemed bored and the redhead who looked bright-eyed.

As for matinee-idol handsome Johnny C, he had broad shoulders or anyway the tux did, an average-size guy who seemed taller. Johnny had shiny black curls that sat on his head like a Roman council, and a black beauty mark of a mole near sensuous lips, adding to a generally debauched air. The long dark eyelashes and dark brown blinkers were part of that, too. Then there were the ruffled cuffs and bejeweled fingers, plus that dark complexion—not a tan, a gift from Mommy and Daddy back in Sicily.

Book-ending the booth, seated on the outside next to the redhead and blonde, were two outsize bodyguards. Like the pug-ugly doorman at the Waldorf, this matched pair dressed really well for hoods. Not tuxes like the boss, though, or tweeds either. But decent charcoal suits with sharp dark-blue silk ties, even if their rods did bulge.

One hood, seated next to the blonde, had an interesting decorative touch around his thick neck—purple and yellow bruises, splotchy things. Like the kind that got made when somebody was choking you and really putting some effort into it. I had never seen this boy, a tiny-eyed sort with a hook nose, or his friend, a dimple-chinned specimen with a black burr haircut.

What was interesting was that they were both scowling at me in apparent recognition.

Being a shrewd detective, I deducted more or less immediately that this was the pair who yesterday had rifled my office and scuffled with me in the dark.

"Mike Hammer," Johnny C said in his smooth baritone, lifting his Manhattan as if in a toast. "Isn't El Borracho a little rich for your blood? Or are private detectives in demand for divorce work in our glorious post-war world?"

"I don't do divorce work," I said, yanking over a chair from a nearby table for four, with a nod to a startled couple who could spare it. I sat facing Johnny and jerked a thumb at the tiny-eyed hood and then his dimple-chin partner. "Maybe I came for the two-headed fish."

The goons frowned at this, but Johnny chuckled. Speaking of private eyes, the redhead was giving me one, slipping me a wink when Johnny wasn't looking. You'd think she would prefer the Don Juan who brung her to a rough apple like yours truly.

"What did you come for, Mr. Hammer?" Johnny C asked, his ripe lips smiling but his eyes cold.

I reached in my suit coat pocket and got out the scented hanky and tossed it on the table. It landed right in front of him and he frowned down at it.

"I've spent a couple days trying to find out who Sharron Wesley's silent partner was," I said, "and all this time the answer was in my pocket. I found that hanky in a money cage at the casino. I figured it for a lady's because of the delicate work and the scent. But that 'G' on it stands for Giovanni… Italian for John."

Johnny C said nothing. The smile was gone, the cold eyes remained.

I sipped my rye and soda. "Maybe it *is* a 'lady's' hanky. Maybe you sleep with Frick and Frack here, and the dollies are just window dressing."

Now the blonde was smiling at me, too. Pay dirt.

"I don't really give a damn either way," I said, "but Sharron Wesley sure as hell wasn't your moll. I don't think she was your partner, either. You had her under your thumb. She lived in a little apartment in her own mansion, and played hostess on weekends and bag woman on week-days."

Johnny C shrugged, reclaimed the hanky and stuck it away somewhere. "Joe, Tony... show Mr. Hammer outside. In the alley. I'll join you shortly. I'd like to have a private talk with him."

Both hoods grinned at their boss, nodded, then grinned at me.

"I'm game," I said, getting up.

Both girls were frowning now, possibly in concern or maybe because the floor show was over. I just let Joe and Tony guide me by either arm across the dance floor to a side door onto the alley.

It was no darker out there than in El Borracho. Tony shut the door on the nightclub noises and city sounds took over, like the yell Joe let out when I sent my heel into his knee, sharp and hard. Joe's grip on my arm was gone and I swung around to face Tony, whose tiny little eyes got as wide as they could and I head-butted him in his hooked nose.

Then Tony's grip was gone, too—he was busy dealing with twin streams of blood from flared nostrils. Thanks to his hurting knee, Joe was kneeling like he was about to receive communion, but what he got was a roundhouse right hand that turned his mouth into a red foamy thing spitting teeth like seeds and he went down all the way, his hands covering his face with more red squirting between his fingers. Tony was trying to recover, still on his feet but wobbly, his lower face a mask of scarlet. I figured he needed some rest, too, like his pal, and sunk a fist into his gut so deep that puking was his only option. That, and tottering till he fell, doing a nasty belly-flop on the bricks. Joe was holding up red-smeared palms, begging for mercy, or anyway I think he was—you couldn't make out much from the bubbling froth.

I might consider mercy for Joe, but at the moment I

was busy bringing back a foot to kick Tony in the face when the door opened and Johnny C stepped out, his easy smile turning to horror-struck alarm as he saw the bloody mess his fallen angels were making.

"*Don't*, Hammer! You'll kill him! *Please!*"

I didn't figure a kick in the head would kill the punk, but it might have, and Johnny *had* said please.

The too-handsome gambling czar rushed over, his eyes white all the way round, making a stark contrast with his head of black Roman curls. He was gesturing with both hands, pleading.

"Ye gods, Hammer! I really just wanted to talk in private! There was no need for this."

"You should have been more clear," I said with a shrug, digging out a ruined deck of Luckies and fingering out a semblance of a cigarette. "Anyway, those two shook down my office yesterday. And they handed me my tail. So I handed theirs back."

"They're just doing their job!"

"Yeah, that's what the Nazis said." I stuffed the rumpled cigarette in my mouth and got it going somehow. "Why have my office tossed, Johnny? What did I ever do to you?"

He sighed. His boys were providing background music with their whimpering. Actually, Joe was weeping. Their boss glanced at them with concern. Maybe he did sleep with them.

Then he turned to me, calm as the spring breeze that was playing with refuse in the alley. "Hammer, I have friends in Sidon… in official circles."

"No kidding."

"I heard you were poking around into the Sharron Wesley killing. I have my own interests in that matter."

I blew smoke at him. "There wasn't a murder case

when I went out there. The dead woman didn't even turn up till the day after I arrived. Of course, she was dead a week already. Maybe you knew that."

He shook his head. "No. I had nothing to do with her murder—she was the last person I wanted to see dead. I had reason to believe she'd been holding out on me. That she had a great deal of my money hidden away somewhere."

I frowned at that. "Didn't you own the casino together?"

He shook his head. He dug a silver cigarette case and got out his own cigarette. It wasn't rumpled, but I gave him a light, anyway.

"Sidon was strictly *my* operation," he said.

"But it was her place! Her mansion! What happened to the cool million she inherited?"

He drew smoke in through his sly smile. "Oh, a lot of that money went into the set-up, all right. She just didn't have a piece of it."

"What the hell did you have on her, Johnny? Evidence that she killed old E.J. Wesley? Or maybe you bought the jurors. Is that it, jury-rigging? Maybe it wasn't Sharron's long legs that got her acquitted, but your long green."

That sly smile turned downright decadent. "Does it matter, Mike? May I call you Mike? I'd like us to be friends."

He put a bejeweled hand on my shoulder and I picked it off like a gaudy insect that had lit there.

"We'll keep it friendly," I allowed. "But I'm particular about choosing my friends. What's on your mind, Johnny? What the hell was going on out there that has you and Dekkert and the entire Sidon city government doing handstands?"

He thought about those questions for a while. Clearly he was making a decision. He'd said he wanted me to be his friend. But what I thought he really wanted was me as an ally.

I was right.

"Mike," he said, "you're probably aware Sharron delivered our weekend take to me, in cash, regularly. We did it discreetly, playing into her reputation as a sort of party girl, and mine as a Romeo."

And both had been a façade.

"She was never really my 'moll,'" he said, quietly amused. "She was strictly a bag man, or bag woman, if you prefer. I paid her well. I wasn't a cruel partner."

"You weren't a partner at all. You were her boss."

"Yes. Yes, you're right, and that was the problem, wasn't it?"

"Was it?"

He nodded, and his smile turned into a sour twitch. "She was skimming from me. For how long, I have no damn idea, but she was skimming. I believe she was building a sort of stake that would be enough for her to leave the country, and live comfortably, starting anew, under another name."

"And out from under your thumb, huh? That makes sense. She wasn't keeping *all* the money then—she was giving you enough to fool you, for a while, anyway—but the skim over a period of months, or even a year, that could really add up."

"Yes. Yes, it could. We're both lucky, you and I, that Sidon has the corrupt police force it does. A real murder investigation, conducted by the state police, would mean that mansion and those grounds would be turned upside down. My money would be found, and confiscated."

"Do you think the Sidon cops are wise to Sharron's money stash?"

He quickly shook his head. "I don't see how they could

be… but they *could* blunder onto it."

I raised an eyebrow. "If Dekkert doesn't know there was a hoard of cash stashed out there, why was he so hot to find out what became of Sharron Wesley? He damn near beat a little beachcomber to death, just because the guy lived close enough to the Wesley place to have seen something."

Johnny sucked in deep on the cigarette holder, and when he finally exhaled, smoke floated skyward like a new Pope had been picked. "You may be right, Mike. Dekkert may have gotten wise. All the more reason for me to enlist your help."

"What do you have in mind?"

He leaned closer. He smelled like that hanky. "If you can find the stashed skim money, you can have yourself a fat finder's fee. Twenty-five percent."

"You wouldn't be trying to distract me now, would you, Johnny?"

He scowled. "You know damn well I didn't kill the Wesley woman! I wanted her alive, to find out where she hid what she stole from me. So your search for her killer will *not* lead to me."

Damn. I believed him.

"If you don't find the money," he went on, with a casual shrug, "or if someone beats you to it, I will still pay your daily rate."

"All right," I said. "Fifty a day. I cover my own expenses."

"Very generous of you, Mike. We'll start that rate as of yesterday, as a gesture to make up for what happened at your office. Mea culpa."

"Yeah. Your culpa, all right."

That pretty boy mug of his dealt me a seductive, hood-eyed gaze. "Could you help with one other item, Mr. Hammer?"

"Uh, what's that?"

He nodded toward his two boys, who had managed to get themselves into sitting positions against the side of the building, their legs sticking straight out.

"I'd like to get Joe and Tony to a hospital. Could you help me convey them to my car?"

What the hell—why not?

That took only five minutes, and then I was on my way back to Sidon.

The pieces were coming together now. I didn't know if I could lay hands on Johnny C's skim money. But I would soon have a killer in my grasp, or on the end of my rod.

Either way, I'd be squeezing.

CHAPTER ELEVEN

By the time I rolled into Sidon, it was damn near midnight. The long day was getting to me again and I'd almost nodded off a couple of times behind the wheel, thanks to the endless gray ribbon of highway cutting down the Island.

Best thing now was to sit down with Velda, compare notes and make a game plan for tomorrow. With what I'd learned in the city, and whatever she picked up at that roadhouse, we'd be ready to head down the home stretch.

But at the Sidon Arms, when I called her room from the house phone, I got no answer. That didn't raise a red flag, since I'd dispatched her to gather intelligence at the hotel's cocktail lounge and that jive-jumping roadhouse. So it would be no surprise if she got back well after midnight.

I was heading up the stairs with the intent of hitting the rack good and hard when a hoarse male voice called out: "Mike! Hold up there!"

I turned and saw Doc Moody, looking desperate and disheveled, stumbling out of the bar, trying to work up some speed. He was flushed and his hands were clawing at the air, like he was trying to climb an invisible ladder.

He met me at the bottom of the stairs, his white hair askew, his eyes wide and red behind the wire-rim glasses. Not surprisingly, he smelled like he'd fallen into a beer vat.

"Poochie's *gone*, Mike! *Gone!* They *grabbed* him!"

Moody wasn't slurring—in fact he was over-enunciating—and he was more upset than drunk. But he was drunk enough.

I could have slapped the old fool, but instead I kept my head and said, "Slow it down, Doc. Come on. Let's sit over here and you tell me all about it."

I walked him over to a threadbare couch and we sat. A droopy potted plant next to him seemed to eavesdrop.

His voice was breathy and rushed. "Mike, I just stepped out for a minute… just to… just to run an *errand*…"

His breath made evident just what kind of errand he had run.

"I've been keeping Poochie in my little spare room… nice little quiet room… and he's hardly stuck his nose out. He's been scared, Mike. So goddamn scared of Dekkert and his bunch. I told him he could listen to my radio, he could go fix himself food in the kitchen, any time he wanted, but no, he'd just stay in that little spare room. I'd take his meals in on trays and—"

"Doc, skip the crap. What happened?"

He was shaking his head, close to hysteria. "I've been waiting for you to get back. Waiting and watching."

From the hotel bar.

"The point, Doc. Get to the point."

"About…"

He looked at his wrist watch and did a comic routine,

trying to make his eyes focus, that would have been a riot if this were goddamn burlesque.

"...about an *hour* ago. Little more. I come back from that... that errand? I come back, gone an hour, maybe two, and that little spare room, it was topsy-turvy. Everything turned upside down. And he was gone! Poochie was gone."

Damn.

I asked, "Did the room look like it had been searched? Drawers sticking out, closet in disarray? Were they *looking* for something?"

"No! They were looking for *Poochie*! The mess was from a struggle. From them *taking* him. Mike, there was blood on the floor."

"How much blood?"

"Drops. Just drops. They didn't beat him or kill him at my place, I don't think... they just, just *took* him..."

"Who took him?"

He shook his head, ashamed. "I don't know. It *has* to be the police, doesn't it? Dekkert and his thugs?"

I nodded glumly.

The red rheumy eyes were full of tears. "Mike, I'm sorry, Mike... I let you down. I didn't *mean* to let you down..."

"It's all right," I said. "You just go on home. No more drinking, Doc, not tonight. Just go home, get some rest. I'll let you know tomorrow how it came out. I'll want you clear-eyed then, okay?"

"Yes, Mike... yes..."

He was sitting there when I left, just a dejected slumped shape in a rumpled suit, with his white hair ruffled, his glasses crooked on a blood-shot nose that was a sorry beacon in his grooved yet puffy face, while his red eyes stared into nothing.

If anybody was to blame here, though, it was me. Me

for entrusting Poochie's care to an old rummy like the Doc, and not keeping closer tabs on both jailer and his charge. Not that I'd had a lot of options in Sidon among people I could trust.

But another on that short list was Big Steve.

I flew out of the front door of the hotel into a night that had turned chilly with breeze enough to make me tug down my hat and turn up my collars. It was like winter was changing its mind about letting spring take over, and summer was out of the question.

What was good about the temperature drop was how it woke me up, slapped me to alertness, not that the Doc's news about Poochie hadn't already done that. I crossed a street devoid of traffic and headed for the diner on the way to the police station. I got out the .45, flicked off the safety and racked one into the chamber. The idea was to see if Big Steve wanted to back my play—I wasn't sure how many cops would be on duty at the station, and I planned to go in there hard and heavy.

That Pollack hated the corruption in his town, and I would bet my back teeth he had a weapon handy to take to the party, whether a sawed-off or a baseball bat. And he had sons, sons as big as he was, who might wade in with me.

I would be checking every alleyway as I went, but my idea was that right now Poochie would be in a back room of the Sidon station, getting the classic Third Degree treatment, rubber hose and all. I would feed that rubber hose to Dekkert, and kick Chiefie's ass to Kingdom Come…

But as I neared the diner, which blazed with lights indicating it was still open, despite the hour, I saw through the long wide windows two figures in blue uniforms seated at the counter, the only customers. I saw Big Steve, too, down the counter, minding his own business, wiping away with a rag.

And even turned away from me, those two blue backsides could only belong to Sidon's top-ranking excuses for police—Chief Beales and Deputy Dekkert.

That stopped me so cold in my tracks I damn near fell on my face. It was highly unlikely these two exemplars of the law would have grabbed Poochie from the doc's, then gone to the diner for a bite while letting somebody else handle the back-room interrogation.

What the hell?

Wind whispering in my ears but not making its message plain, I eased the .45 back under my arm but left the coat unbuttoned as I went up the couple of steps into the box-car diner. I settled onto the stool next to the chief, with Dekkert next to him.

As if I didn't notice who my counter mates were, I called out, "So this is a twenty-four-hour joint, huh, Steve?"

Big Steve gave me a grin that lifted his black handlebar mustache halfway to his eyes. As he turned to wring out his rag in the sink, he said, "Open till midnight, Mike. Not closing for another five minutes. Fix you up with a burger or a dog maybe?"

"I'll have a slice of that apple pie and some coffee."

"Comin' right up, my friend."

Both Chief Beales and Dekkert were giving me frozen sideways glances. Theirs were the kind of open-yapped expression the driver of a car wears when he sees the truck about to hit him head on.

"Gentlemen," I said with a friendly nod. "Little late for the town's top cops to be finishing up a shift, isn't it?"

Neither said a word. They still just looked at me, Beales with popping eyes in that fat thick-lipped face of his, bullet-headed Dekkert staring out of eyes like small black buttons sewn on his face. Funny—seeing me made Beales turn red and Dekkert white, almost as white as the half-dozen bandages that seemed haphazardly applied to that once handsome face his blobby nose had ruined.

Those bandages were smaller than when last I'd seen Dekkert, but still a nice reminder of what I'd done to him in that alley. And later at the police station.

As genial as Fibber McGee, I said, "I was just on my way over to the station to report a crime."

The chief licked the fat lips, but it was Dekkert who snapped, "*What* crime?"

"That little beachcomber you boys took such a shine to—he's been recovering at Doc Moody's from a gunshot wound. He caught a bullet through the open window of his shack last Saturday night."

The chief's frown consisted of ridges of furrowed fat. "What are you *saying*, Hammer? Is *that* the crime you're reporting?"

I shook my head.

Big Steve delivered my coffee and pie.

Stirring some sugar into the java, I said absently, "No, I didn't bother reporting that. You see, I'm pretty sure it was your deputy here that shot Poochie, so calling it in struck me as redundant."

Dekkert flushed around the white bandages and blurted, "I did *not* do no such thing! Watch your mouth, Hammer! Accusations like that can get your ass hauled in."

"I didn't say I was *sure* you did it," I said, shoveling in a bite of pie. It would have been better warm, but it was still good. "Anyway, I was the intended target, not Poochie."

The chief swallowed. He tried to fill his chest with indignation but it looked like so much more flab to me.

"Maybe my deputy is right, Mr. Hammer. Maybe we *should* go over to the station, and take down your statement."

"Here's my statement. Poochie's been lying low at Doc Moody's, recuperating from that bullet wound, not to mention the beating you devoted servants of the law gave him. I figure keeping the little guy with Moody was kosher since he is, after all, your local coroner."

Dekkert spat, "He won't be for long!"

I chewed, swallowed, washed it down. "That's your business. I don't mess in local politics. The thing is, somebody has grabbed Poochie out of the doc's place. Looks to have been a struggle."

The chief demanded, "When was this?"

"An hour ago at least. Not more than a few hours ago at most."

"Was Doc Moody there when Poochie was taken?"

"Nah. He was out drinking somewhere. Anyway, what I need to know is…" I wiped off my mouth delicately with a paper napkin and then gave them my worst goddamn grin. "…was it *you*?"

I watched their reactions. The chief seemed honestly confused, and frankly so did Dekkert.

With a half-spin on the stool, I turned to face them with the suit coat hanging open, revealing that big nasty gun under my arm.

"Well, Chiefie?"

But he was already shaking his head. "No, Hammer, I don't know anything about this." He looked back at his deputy. "If *you* know something about this, Deputy Dekkert—"

"I *don't*," Dekkert said insistently, but it was the movement in his eyes—the fast, even desperate thinking he was doing—that made me believe him.

The chief seemed genuinely astounded. "Why would

anybody want to kidnap Poochie? Why him of all people?"

I grunted a laugh. "Well, you local cops were interested enough in him the other day."

The chief slammed a fat fist on the counter and my pie jumped. "Hammer, that was before Sharron Wesley turned up dead! We wanted to know if he'd seen anything on that beach. We were looking for any lead we could find."

I studied him some more. "The disappearance of Sharron Wesley was troubling to you, wasn't it, Chiefie? A lot was at stake. Plenty of local income, particularly off-season, depended on that dizzy dame."

The chief shrugged. "Why should I deny it?" He cleared his throat rather theatrically. "Hammer, I'm going over to the station and I'm calling everybody in. The entire department, back on duty."

What, all six?

He hopped off the stool like a big toad off a medium toadstool. "We'll put out an All Points Bulletin on Poochie, or I should say Stanley Cootz. That's his name. Whatever you may think of us, Mr. Hammer, know this—we run a safe community, safe for the citizens and safe for the visitors who we depend upon during the season. The Sidon PD will *not* sit still for having a serious crime like kidnapping take place in our jurisdiction."

And he tipped his cap to Big Steve, probably in lieu of payment, then waddled out.

Dekkert, on the other hand, did seem to "sit still" for a crime like kidnapping. At least he was still sitting there. He was apparently ignoring his chief's clarion call.

I slid over next to him as Big Steve cleared away a pile of dishes—Chiefie had had an appetite.

"Can you think of any reason," I said, not putting even an ounce of menace into it, "why anybody would kidnap that beachcomber?"

Dekkert shook his head. He seemed to be staring at the open window onto the kitchen, where one of Big Steve's big sons was cleaning up. But I had a feeling Dekkert wasn't seeing much of anything but his own private thoughts. Private thoughts I would like to shake out of him.

But I had a different idea about how to handle this son of a bitch.

"Listen," I said. "Let's let Big Steve close up the joint for the night. We can go over to the hotel bar, find a quiet booth, and have a friendly talk."

His scowl made his bandages shift. "Why the hell would I want to do that?"

"Because you used to be a cop in New York City. You're not just another one of these hicks. You know what's really going on around Sidon, which interests me. And I think *you* might be interested in hearing about what I've turned up lately."

He thought about that.

Finally, he nodded at me, and left his own dirty dishes behind but tossed a quarter on the counter next to the buck I'd left. Whether that was a tip or his idea of payment, I couldn't hazard a guess. Big Steve didn't look thrilled either way.

Outside, I stuffed a smoke in my face and fired it up. I offered him a Lucky and he accepted it. Unlike the chief, he wore no cap, and within that butch cut didn't have enough hair for the breeze to riffle it. The wind would have taken my hat if I hadn't really snugged it down, and it snatched the smoke away from both our cigarettes, making vapor trails as we walked down the middle of a street in a town that would bustle in a few weeks. Right now it was deader than Sharron Wesley.

I said, "I was over in Wilcox the other day."

"Yeah?"

"You know a guy named Dave Miles?"

"Naw."

"Head of security at the brick factory."

"Don't know him."

"I also talked to Sheriff Jackson."

"Him I know."

"Talked to Chief Chasen."

"Him I know, too."

"There's a theory we three kicked around that the Wesley murder might be the work of the same maniac who killed those two college girls in Wilcox. And also that other young gal found strangled on the beach between Sidon and there."

We were outside the hotel now. Wind whipped at his dark-blue blouse and my suit coat, flapping them like flags.

"Those college girls," he said. "They were killed with a knife. Not choked, right?"

"Right."

"And that other one, the girl on the beach? Wasn't she strangled with a nylon?"

"Right again."

Dekkert shrugged his big shoulders. "Sharron was strangled with powerful hands, not a stocking. And I don't see what those girls in that barn have to do with anything."

"There are similarities. All three cases, including the Wesley dame, involved young women—good-looking ones—murdered and left naked, their clothes never found."

The deputy seemed to be mulling that as he sucked up smoke, then exhaled and let the wind whip it away. "Sharron wasn't that young, though."

I grinned. "Yeah, but she wasn't old. She was under forty and still a beauty. You knew her, right?"

He shrugged again. "I don't know anything about those other cases, Hammer, if that's why you brung it up. Out of our jurisdiction."

"Yeah, each kill in a different jurisdiction. Confuses the issue, muddies the waters, don't you think? Somebody's smart. Or knows enough about how law enforcement works to think of spreading his hobby around."

Dekkert was frowning. It made the half-dozen bandages crinkle and bulge. "Is that an accusation?"

I raised my hands in a peace-keeping fashion. "No, just an observation. Buy you a drink?"

He was still frowning.

I made myself smile at him. Not nasty at all. "Come on. Bury the hatchet. Two old ex-New York PD coppers having a nightcap. Couple other points we should discuss... about your friend Sharron."

"What?"

"You don't call her Mrs. Wesley or the Wesley woman or the Wesley dame, I notice. You call her Sharron. You said you knew her. Let's talk about that."

He sneered at me. His fists were bunched. He was getting tired of this. So was I, but I needed to keep this thing friendly. "Why the hell should I, Hammer?"

"Because," I said, and pitched the butt sparking into the night, "I think you might like to know what *I* know."

That he thought about, too, but not for long. He just nodded, and gestured for me to go inside first. I shook my head and gestured for him to do that. I might be playing nice with him but I wasn't going to turn my back, not on this bastard.

"Give me a second," I said, in the lobby.

He stood impatiently while I tried Velda on the house phone. Still no answer. I hung up and nodded toward the bar, and we walked over there.

Soon, in a back booth, with beers in front of both us, and fresh cigs going, we started our friendly chat.

"I was in New York this evening," I said, "and ran into Johnny C. You know, Johnny Casanova?"

Dekkert couldn't have cut it at that table in the Waldorf suite—his was anything but a poker face, eyes tightening and even twitching at the mention of the gambling chieftain.

"Seems he was Sharron Wesley's silent partner," I went on. "Actually more than silent partner—he owns the place. She was a front. Apparently he has something on her, and bled her out of her fortune and even her mansion. He was just letting her live there in a few meager rooms in return for playing hostess. Also, bag woman. But still just another employee."

"I don't know anything about that."

I figured he was lying, but I wouldn't press it—not just yet.

"Dekkert, what was your role out there at the casino? I've heard it said you were a bouncer, but I can't imagine a guy of your gifts would be satisfied with a crummy menial job like that."

His eyes were hard and dark and barely blinking. "Well, Hammer, you're wrong. That's all I did out there—just some security. When I was off-duty. Like cops do."

Then he drank about half his beer in one gulp.

"Okay," I said, "but I've known you for a long time, Deputy Dekkert. You are nothing if not shrewd. Johnny C's role out there, you'd pick up on that. Sharron Wesley's unhappiness, her resentment against Casanova, you'd pick up on that, too."

"So what?"

"So I think there's a cache of money somewhere in that mansion or anyway on that property. It might be as little as the last weekend's take, which would still be plenty. But it might be more."

"More, huh?"

"A lot more. If Sharron was skimming, for example. Planning to take a powder to a better life, maybe down where the mambo is a local dance. But the thing is, sooner or later, Johnny C is gonna come out Sidon way, looking for that dough."

A tiny sneer. "How does he even know there *is* any dough?"

"Oh, he knows. I don't know how, but he told me tonight, so he knows. And when the heat dies down, and there's no chance of running into coppers crawling around the Wesley grounds, Johnny C will come after what he considers rightly his."

Dekkert slugged down the rest of the beer and pushed away the mug, then set his balled fists down like mallets. "Did *he* do it? Did Casanova kill her?"

There was rage in that once-handsome, bandage-spotted face. He cared about Sharron Wesley. Was that why he'd gone ape on Poochie when she was missing? Not the money, or anyway not just the money... but love? Had our boy Dekkert been just another love-sick calf?

"No, Johnny didn't murder her," I said. "And he didn't have her bumped, either. Anyway, I don't think so. That would be killing the golden goose before the egg got laid. He would have questioned her... you know what *kind* of questioning, Dekkert, old pal. The kind you subjected that little beachcomber to."

"But she wasn't beaten," he said hollowly.

"No. She was strangled. And you don't strangle somebody you're trying to make talk."

He nodded slowly. "So what are *you* after, Hammer?"

"I figure you know that property better than anybody.

You worked out there. You knew Sharron. Maybe we could turn up that dough together."

He grunted a laugh. "What, a midnight snipe hunt? Forget it. I did work out there, sure, and I knew her a little. She was a nice broad. We had some fun, time to time. But I never saw any sign she was tied up with Johnny C. And I don't believe she was stealing money. It was her own place, not his, as far as I know. She took the cash into the city and banked it, is the way I understand it. That's the beginning and end of it, Hammer. Okay?"

I shrugged. "Okay. It was worth a try."

He slid out of the booth. "Word of advice, Hammer?"

"Always appreciated," I said pleasantly.

"Get the hell out of Sidon." His upper lip curled all the way back over big front teeth and feral incisors "There's nothing here for you. Not answers. Not money. Not even a good time. *Nothing*."

He stalked out of there. Didn't bother to offer to pay for the beers, but then cops didn't seem to pay for anything around Sidon.

I sat there grinning. Well, he had taken the bait. I'd known damn well he wouldn't go partners with me on the stashed cash, but he would want to beat Johnny C to the punch. So all I had to do was go out to Sharron Wesley's and stake the place out and wait for Dekkert to lead me to the treasure.

Who had grabbed Poochie, I couldn't say. But it really didn't feel like the cops were responsible, and I talked myself into the chief meaning it when he said he'd round up his troops and put on a search for the little guy.

Right now the thread I was following was Dekkert, and it would lead to that cash. I wasn't sure if finding Sharron Wesley's getaway fund would lead me to her murderer, too, but I had a hunch it would.

Anyway, I didn't mind the idea of taking a twenty-five percent finder's fee from Johnny C. No, not at all. I had no other client in this case, and Velda would smile, seeing that kind of fee heading into our bank account.

Speaking of Velda, I tried her again on the house phone, got nothing, and decided to go up to my room to see if she'd left a note under my door or anything.

Nothing.

I was almost back out the door, to stake out the Wesley mansion, when the phone rang.

"Mike?"

It was Velda.

"Finally!" I said. "I've been back since midnight, and do I have plenty to report."

"Tell me about it!" She sounded breathless; I could hear the rustle of wind in trees, so she must be calling from outside somewhere. "Mike, Mayor Rudy Holden has just been killed."

"*What?*"

"You heard me. One shot behind the ear while he sat in his study. He—"

Her voice broke off with a muffled sound as though someone had slapped a hand over her mouth.

"Velda!... Velda, what's wrong? Where *are* you, honey? Answer me!"

The only response I got was the click of the receiver being slung back in its cradle.

I dialed the operator and barked an order at her. "I just had a call. I need to know where it came from. Hurry!"

"I'm sorry, sir," she said with whiny high-pitched indifference. "We can't give out that in-for-*may*-shun." I was boiling. Velda in trouble, and some little snip wouldn't get me the lead I needed.

"Damn it," I yelled, "you'll give that me *right now*, or I'll come down where you work and slap the goddamn hell out of you. Get me that number and its location! This is detective Mike Hammer speaking, and I don't want any crap out of you."

It was a booth three blocks away.

CHAPTER TWELVE

The receiver dangled on its cord, swaying just a little, the violence of the interrupted conversation leaving behind a pendulum that, in the several minutes after the cut-off call, had dissipated to a gentle swing. Like a hanged man after the impact of that sudden fall had worn off.

The phone booth was on the northern edge of the business district, and just around the corner, two blocks down, was the nicest house in town, the red-brick dwelling of the late Mayor Rudolph Holden. Two Sidon police cars with their red lights flashing were parked down there, and even at this distance I could see figures in blue moving in and out of the Holden home.

Velda had said His Honor had "just been killed." Had she been at the murder scene? Maybe discovered the body? In any case, she had been one of the first to know and rushed to call me.

Had the murderer seen her at the scene, and followed her to that phone booth, and put a muffling hand over her mouth to haul her away to… what? Silence her? Nowhere around the booth was there an alley or doorway to lay down an unconscious body with even the most minimal concealment. I looked at every possibility half a block in either direction.

Why had she been taken? Who had taken her? Probably the mayor's murderer, but… *why?* To kill her, assault her, use her as a hostage? *What?*

The night was even colder now and the wind picking up. I cut through it like a blade as I ran down to where those red lights flashed, holding my hat onto my head, my open suit coat flapping like wings and if I could have flown, I would. First the beachcomber, now Velda—why? *Who?*

The two cops who'd backed up Dekkert in that alley at the start were standing on the open, poured-cement porch—that former high school athlete and his skinny pal. They started to say something as they tried to bar the door but I shoved them aside with either hand, hard enough that the skinny one tumbled off in a pile.

Stairs yawned ahead, and off to the right was a living room where on a Victorian sofa an older female relative or maybe family friend sat holding onto one of the new widow's hands with both of hers. Mrs. Holden was weeping into a hanky. Whatever that husband of hers had been, I understood her grief. It was what my rage would turn into if I couldn't get Velda back.

Another cop yelled, "Hey! There's no entry here!"

But I brushed by him into the study where the mayor and I had once eaten sugar cookies.

Chief Beales saw me enter as two cops caught up with me and took me by the arms and I was getting ready to do something about that when Beales said, "It's all right! It's all right. Let go of him. Let him go!"

They did, and moved off growling, not knowing how

lucky they were, and I went over to Beales, who was hovering over the corpse slumped in its chair by the cold fireplace. The mayor was in a purple silk robe with pajamas and slippers, the picture of casual comfort but for the black hole behind his left ear. The hole at the right side of the top of his skull was larger, ragged and red, like an angry whore's mouth.

This wasn't the work of any Jack the Ripper maniac like the one Pat pictured for the kills of the coeds, the Wilson girl and Sharron Wesley. This was an execution, syndicate style. Professional killing hung in the air with the smell of cordite.

Chief Beales looked at me and for once that fat face wasn't flushed, but pale as a blister. His eyes were terrified and his forehead was a bas relief map of pulsing veins.

"What do you think, Mr. Hammer?"

"I think he's dead. What do you think? Who called this in?"

"Mrs. Holden. She and her husband were in bed, reading, and someone rang the doorbell, maybe twenty minutes ago. Her husband went down to answer it, and a few minutes later, she heard the gunshot and went down to check. The front door was open."

So the mayor knew the killer. Invited him or her in to the study for a friendly chat that had prematurely concluded with a gunshot of considerable caliber. .38 anyway, judging by that gaping exit wound.

I said tightly, "What are you going to do about this?"

He was shaking his head in wide-eyed confusion; he didn't look much better than the mayor, who at least seemed to be resting.

"I don't know, Mr. Hammer. I honestly don't know. I may have to ask the state police for help. Things are really getting out of hand."

"Where's your deputy? Dekkert's got real big-city police training. Why isn't he here?"

"He doesn't answer his phone at home and I can't raise him on his radio."

That was because the bastard was already on his way out to the Wesley mansion, if he wasn't there already. Had Dekkert done this? A mob-style hit was something I wouldn't put past him. Had he grabbed Poochie, because the little guy saw something? What? Had Dekkert strangled Sharron on the beach and Poochie witnessed it? Had that sadistic son of a bitch Dekkert thrill-killed all those girls, too? Had he grabbed Velda because she had put the puzzle pieces together before I could, or maybe he snatched her just to gain control over me!

"Hammer!" Beales said. "I'm *talking* to you. What do you think this killing means?"

"It means you better call Sergeant Price," I said, recalling the name of the state cop Pat had vouched for. "And tell the state boys my secretary Velda is missing. And Stanley Cootz."

"Your secretary? Is she the woman staying at the hotel with you?"

"Yes. She's also a licensed private detective. She was doing some investigating here in Sidon while I was following up leads in the city."

"What kind of investigating?"

"Well, she went out to the Hideaway tonight, and if you can spare one of your stalwart law enforcers to go out there and ask around, I'd be grateful."

He nodded. "I'll send two men out. There's only so much for us to do here, goddamnit." A jagged vein in his nose was throbbing. "What are *you* going to do?"

"I'm going to find Velda."

"Your secretary? How?"

I didn't bother answering that, just blew out of there

and ran through the increasingly chilly night back to the hotel parking lot, where I fired up the heap and headed out to the casino. Never had the champion engine in that loser of a jalopy ever served me better, hitting eighty in seconds with the body shaking as if it shared the fear and rage I felt. The front windows were down and cold air churned, bringing in ocean smells.

Ninety.

Clouds were gliding like ghosts over a full moon whose beauty seemed mocking as glimpsed through the eerily waving trees, leaves shimmering, trunks bending, terrible monstrous shapes doing a pagan sacrificial dance.

One hundred.

Then I eased off because the cutoff leading to the Wesley house was up ahead, and I didn't want to overshoot. I took the curve at forty and the rubber whined and the buggy leaned, but then we were there.

The iron gate stood open and the plantation-like mansion loomed on its man-made hillock, catching the moon's ivory rays and holding onto them, until shifting cloud cover turned it temporarily into a silhouette, before an almost phosphorescent glow returned. Again, I drove only halfway up the drive before pulling over to park in the bushes off to the right. Up the driveway, blocking the way, was a police car.

Unlike the two Sidon squads parked outside the mayor's place, this cruiser did not have its red light flashing. This was Dekkert's ride, and it was no surprise he'd brought a city vehicle out here, and not his personal car, because this way his presence at the mansion could be explained by his official status.

Only I knew damn well this was an unofficial visit.

I felt confident I knew where he was headed. No lights were on in the mansion, not even the shifting beam of a flashlight. No, Dekkert was not inside. I'd gone over that place stem to stern already, with no safe to be found.

Then I saw movement over by the house, and wondered if I'd misjudged. But at that moment the moon came out from behind clouds to drench the mansion in a pale glow that revealed the movement to be a few scrawny cats checking out empty, overturned garbage cans.

No. Nobody in the house.

The rod was in my right hand, a round chambered, safety off, as I pushed through the bushes and stayed low, crossing the open ground that led to the row of trees that served as a high fence discouraging neighbors and beach worshipers. The trees began on solid ground that got progressively sandy until their roots were reaching under the beach in search of soil, and I was near the edge of the water. My ears were filled with the sibilant sound of ocean swells stirred by wind to rush the shore.

But I heard something else, too.

A metallic click and then the screechy whine of wood on cement.

I moved between the last few trees and saw the white-painted Victorian structure, sort of a miniature band shell big enough only to house the padded bench within, the view facing the house not the ocean—the quaintly baroque gazebo where I figured Sharron Wesley must have hidden her horde of cash.

And Dekkert was proving me right.

Still in his police blues, he hunkered his burly frame over as he moved the bench whose hidden latch he'd thrown, swinging it out and over to reveal the safe with combination lock set into the green-painted cement floor. His back was to me as I moved silently on the sand up behind him, stopping at the bottom of the three wooden steps up to the cozy little nook.

Despite the rush of surf, the sounds of him turning that dial, not just the grinding whirr but even the tiny clicks, were easy enough to discern. Much more easy to hear was that final clunk of the handle as he unlatched, then lifted the door open.

Though his back was still angled to me, I could tell he was smiling down into the sunken compartment, like Ali Baba regarding a treasure chest of glittering gold and jewels.

"Thanks, Dekkert," I said.

He whipped that bullet head my way and those hard dark eyes damn near popped out of their sockets in a face still patch-worked with bandages. His left hand remained on the handle of the swung-open floor safe. His other hand was outstretched, ready to dip into the stash of cash, but frozen mid-air before it could take the trip.

"Safe-cracking isn't a specialty of mine," I said, starting up the steps, "and you saved me calling in an expert."

That lady killer mug of his, already betrayed by this blobby nose, crinkled now into an ugly mask of hate, buckling the bandages. He jammed his hand down into the safe and I knew at once that a gun was down there—always a smart move keeping a gun in a money-filled save, you know—and my right foot hit the final step while my left foot came down hard on that little iron door and smashed it into his wrist. His shrill scream floated out over the ocean and then I was up there with him, where I stomped on the door again and again until I heard bones shatter and crack.

He blurted hoarse profanities as with the arm attached to the damaged wrist he shoved the safe's door back to where it rested on its hinges, its contents there for the world to see, or anyway for me to see, as I moved closer and gazed down at riches that weren't gold and jewels exactly, but were a damn good second place.

Stacks and stacks of cash: twenties, fifties, hundreds, with identifying bands… and resting on top, a Colt .38 revolver.

"That was optimistic," I said, sitting on the bench, swung to one side.

Dekkert was sitting on the floor of the gazebo in the moonlight, leaning back against some latticework, his hand with its shattered wrist in his lap, cradled by his other hand. He was crying, wrenching sobs coming up out of his big chest in a rhythm that fit perfectly with the wind-driven tide.

"Optimistic," I clarified, "because I already had a gun in my hand, and you had to reach down for that .38 in the safe. I mean, hell's bells—I let you go for your gun back at the station house and *still* out-drew you."

The sobbing was easing. He was either realizing how undignified that cry baby crap was for a tough guy like him, or maybe shock was settling in. Whatever the case, he had recovered his poise enough to start calling me every dirty name in the book.

I let him get that out of his system, then said, "You were Sharron's *real* silent partner. Oh, not in the casino business, no… but in the skim racket. She always had a man in her life, Sharron, needed a broad shoulder to lean on, and maybe somebody with at least half a brain to help her think. But in her bedroom, I saw no sign of male cohabitation. So I figured she had a boyfriend in either Manhattan or maybe even Sidon, possibly somebody married. Anyway, somebody that required discretion. But when you and I had our friendly talk earlier tonight, Dekkert, I saw it in your face, heard it in your voice. You *loved* the dame, didn't you?"

He wasn't cursing me now, but he was crying again.

I didn't figure this crying had anything to do with the busted-up wrist, either. Nor was there whimpering. Just sorrow leaking out of those dark eyes, which didn't seem so hard all of a sudden. When a teardrop hit a bandage, it would skid to a stop, then pearl and plunk to the floor.

"You were who Sharron was planning to run off with, Dekkert. You worked for her out here, under the guise of doing security on your off-duty hours, but it was much more than that. I even know how you rigged the skim. Johnny C almost certainly had employees on staff, keeping an eye on Sharron, making sure she played it straight. I wouldn't be surprised if you weren't the one who came up with the scam, Dekkert."

His eyes tightened, the tears ebbing. He was listening. He wanted to see if I really had it figured out.

"I saw a big box of poker chips in the trunk of Sharron's Caddy," I said. "She didn't have to rig any books, or work any kind of accounting magic. She didn't need to skim any money from the till, not with you playing the shill, cashing in chips at cashier windows and carrying off the cash… for storage later under your little love seat. Wow. How you planned and schemed and dreamed, you crazy kids, like any two lovebirds. And then what happened? What went finally wrong? Did Johnny get wise?"

Dekkert swallowed thickly. "No… no, he never did. But Sharron, after the last party, she… she just disappeared."

"And you went bughouse, beating up that little beachcomber, right? Or did something *else* happen? Did she find another broad shoulder to lean on, another, *better* prospect to run off with, and you killed her in a jealous rage? Strangled the life out of her. And then what—did Poochie see it?… What did you do with him, Dekkert? Where *is* he? Is he dead, too?"

He shook his head. "No. No. No."

I went over and shook him. "No *what*?"

"I... I didn't kill her... I didn't kill Sharron. You're right, you lousy bastard. I loved her. End of the season, we would have been out of here. Gone. There's a quarter of a million in that safe, Hammer. And by season's end, we'd have had another hundred grand, easy. But she disappeared. She really just... disappeared."

I grabbed him by his shirt front, police blue bunching through my fingers. "And Poochie?"

He shrugged and it took effort. "I really just wanted to know if he'd seen anything. He was always hanging around the beach, picking up junk, scrounging in the garbage. He might have seen something."

"So you beat him half to death. Just in case he *saw* something?"

He swallowed again; his eyes were glazing—shock *was* setting in. "I... I... guess I went... went overboard."

"So did your girl Sharron. She was taken out there..." I pointed to the ocean, "...and dumped. But she came back, didn't she? She came back, maybe on a tide like tonight. What do you know about *that*, Dekkert?"

He squinted and tears squirted out. His face was flushed against the white of the bandages. "Nothing... it was awful... awful seeing her like that... draped over that goddamn statue... little holes eaten out of her, bloated and blue, and oh my God, what a nightmare. What a goddamn nightmare."

I stuck the .45 in his throat. "You're saying you *don't* have Poochie."

"No!"

I cocked the .45 and the click made a small sharp but very distinct sound against the surf-tossed night. "What about Velda?"

His red teary eyes were wild now. "Wh-who...?"

"My secretary!"

"The dame… the dame you're with… at the hotel?"

I shook him like a disobedient child. "Yes! Yes! Where the hell *is* she? What have you done with her?"

"Nothing! Nothing! Everything was going to Hell in a handbasket, and with you stirring things up, I decided the best thing was to just… just come out here and grab my money and get the hell out. Cut my damn losses."

I let loose of the slumped figure, and he rocked back against the latticework as I took a step back, straightened. I let down the hammer gently on the .45, and lowered it, the weapon hanging at my side, a useless appendage.

My every instinct told me Dekkert was telling the truth. And if he was, I had just reached the worst kind of dead-end, with Velda gone and no other trail to follow.

But what if Dekkert was the maniac who had killed all those girls and he really did have Velda hidden away somewhere awaiting his sick pleasure, but like so many psychopaths was a dissembler of Satanic proportions? Had he just sold me a convincing bill of goods? Should I beat him half to death to find out, the way he had that dimwit in the alley? Was that how I could find out if he was a mad dog? To viciously tear him apart until I foamed at the mouth and he told me what I wanted to hear, whether it was true or not? Who was the mad dog now?

Then the point became moot because a crack of thunder split the night and I jumped, only it wasn't thunder but a gunshot and a bullet splintered Dekkert's skull, entering his forehead at an angle, between bandages, spraying blood and bone and brain matter on the latticework where it dripped like wet paint. He fell back almost lazily against the framework and one last breath gushed out of him before he went limp, as if sleep had overtaken him, and in a way it had.

"Pitch that rod over on the sand," Johnny Casanova

said, in his smooth baritone, "nice and gentle, Hammer."

The .45 was still hanging at my side. There were three of them—the boss plus the two I'd battered outside El Borracho, back on their feet already but with faces bulging with swollen patches, like they'd run into a hive of bees and had a bad allergic reaction. They could have Dekkert's bandages if they liked—he was through with them. They wore sports shirts and slacks now with car coats. Sharp-looking boys out for some fun on the Island.

Three city boys come to the beach for a party, all with guns pointed at me.

Johnny C—still in his tuxedo but with a camel's hair coat slung around his shoulders, in deference to the wind—pointed a long-barreled .38 my way, probably the gun that had killed Mayor Holden. The other two had automatics, the tiny-eyed, hook-nosed one a nine millimeter, a Browning I thought, and the dimpled-chin character a .38 automatic, probably a Colt. Actually, any one of those weapons could have killed the mayor.

I was damn good with that rod of mine—like I told the late Deputy Dekkert a few days ago, I practiced with it.

But I was facing three guns aimed right at me, and my .45 was hanging in my hand pointing to the gazebo's cement floor. They were maybe ten feet away. I could dive off this thing, and shoot as I did. That might do it. Lousy odds, but odds. Then another idea occurred to me.

So I pitched the gun down to the bottom of the stairs, where it landed soft as silk in the sand. Raised my hands for a moment, Mr. Cooperation, then put them down again and gave the gambling boss a friendly grin.

I said, "We don't have any argument, do we, Johnny? I'm working for you, right? And I found your money, didn't I? How's that for service?"

"And I expected nothing less of you," Johnny said,

moving a little closer. The ivory moonlight caught the Roman curls and glittered off the moisture there. "I figured you'd lead us to it. And you have. My thanks."

"You're welcome. Mind if I go?"

He ignored that, saying, "But as far as you finding it and keeping twenty-five percent for the fee, I wasn't so sure you were serious."

"My reputation is good. I wouldn't have stiffed you."

"Your rep is *too* good. You might not want to work for a syndicate type like me. You are known to have an aversion to my kind of people."

Did he mean gangsters or nancies?

"Still, you're right, Hammer, I have nothing against you. But you *do* find yourself in an unfortunate, severely precarious position."

I let my grin go sly. "You mean, you need somebody to pin the mayor's murder on, and Dekkert's. And I'm handy."

A smile blossomed, moving his black beauty mark an inch farther from gleaming teeth. "That's another aspect of your reputation, Hammer, that I must say is not undeserved. I have heard that you're as smart as you are tough, and that would seem to be the case."

Clouds moving over the moon threw weird shadows, then moments later would wash everything ivory. We were like pale statues oblivious to a world moving quickly around us.

"Why," I said, "because I know you bumped the mayor and now Dekkert? They must have been the only two locals in the know about your connection to this casino. Or is Chief Beales next on the docket?"

"I never dealt with Beales. I'm told he's a fool."

"But *you* aren't a fool, are you, Johnny? You dealt only with those two Sidon officials, the mayor and the former

New York crooked copper who you probably already knew. And you had Sharron Wesley fronting for you. Like all good syndicate bosses, you make sure you are well-insulated from any legal responsibility."

The gambling czar shrugged and his smile traveled to one side of his face. "Being fully 'insulated,' as you so colorfully put it, Hammer, is difficult if not impossible. The investigation into Sharron Wesley's death could well lead back to me... so it's prudent to clean things up, tie off loose ends, and go back to the city."

I grunted a laugh. "Why, won't the Sharron Wesley estate show you as the true owner of that mansion over there—you know, the one with the Vegas-level gambling layout?"

The pretty boy boss was shaking his head, his expression patronizing. "No. My name will not turn up in that fashion. Oh, I do own the Wesley place, but a dummy company I set up is listed as the owner, and plenty of legal paperwork and red tape has been designed to accomplish two things—*hide* my ownership and *retain* my ownership."

"Then at some point you'll re-open."

He nodded. "But not this season. Maybe not even the next. Only when the dust has fully settled. Now, Mr. Hammer, if you'll excuse me, and with my apologies..." He turned to his boys, one on either side. "Joe... Tony... you should probably use *my* gun."

So Johnny had personally killed Mayor Holden. That explained why Rudy had let him into his study as if for just another business meeting.

"Johnny!" I said.

He flashed his gaze back at me with a frown, as if he'd forgotten I was still there—or still alive. As if I were already dead with the mayoral murder gun pressed in my palm. "What is it, Hammer?"

"Did *you* take Velda? Do *you* have her?"

He frowned. "Who in the bloody hell is Velda?"

"My secretary. She's missing."

"Well, isn't that a shame."

He turned toward Tony, apparently about to pass him the murder weapon.

I called out: "And Poochie—what about *him*?"

Now the dapper gangster seemed truly exasperated. Why was he having to answer these questions from an about-to-be corpse?

"Who the hell is Poochie?" he asked irritably.

I smiled. "Sorry, Giovanni. Didn't mean to be a nuisance. Don't you want your money?" I was beside the open safe, and knelt there. "Two hundred-fifty grand down in here, easy. Come on, be fair about it. I found it for you, didn't I? Isn't that worth something?"

Johnny C looked truly annoyed with my still being conversant, let alone alive, and handed the murder gun toward Tony to take care of that, and I reached into the safe, found the .38 and thumbed the safety and brought it up over the open safe door to fire three times in succession, three whip cracks in the night that did nothing at all to silence the surging tide.

But it did a fine job on Johnny C and his boys.

The funny thing was how all three just stood there for a moment, tottering, as if they were wondering why they were still standing, only they weren't wondering anything at all because they were dead, with holes in their foreheads that had exited in a fine spray that left behind little clouds of scarlet to get caught by the ocean breeze and drift away.

I gave the four dead men no further thought. I didn't even bother with the money—that could wait. I just retrieved my .45 and ran into the night, following the only lead, the only hunch I had, and if I was wrong, I knew Velda didn't have a prayer. That she would wash up on this beach some day like Sharron Wesley, if the fish didn't get her first.

CHAPTER THIRTEEN

The waves growled as I moved down the beach, the ocean flicking my face, as if trying to cool me off, as if the chill breeze weren't enough, and maybe it wasn't, because my brain was burning. I moved quickly under a moon displayed by the night sky like a pearl in its navel, winking, then disappearing as the belly dancer's veils of traveling clouds briefly blotted it out. Even the sand didn't slow me, and my vision was keen, I could see every goddamn grain on the ivory-washed beach. But my mind was a blur of rage, hate and frustration.

I had the puzzle pieces, all of them, and the part of the puzzle that concerned Johnny C and Dekkert was complete, off to one side, forming half the picture, finished as far as it went.

But Sharron Wesley remained part of the rest of the puzzle, and the only way I could make those pieces fit was to cut a jigsaw shape to *make* it fit, to force it into a picture-revealing slot even while knowing that another gaping hole would show up all too soon.

As I walked along, lost in thought, I almost stumbled over the thing—the puffy, ravaged body of a dog there on the shore, the waves lapping at it like an eager puppy. A boxer, a big one. Kneeling, holding my breath to avoid the smell of putrefaction, I could see that the animal's neck had been broken.

Sharron Wesley's dog?

I walked on. Had another puzzle piece washed to shore, or just the remains of a red herring?

Something in me knew that the answer lay in a dilapidated shack just down the beach from the Wesley mansion. A hovel put together with washed-up wood, chunks of dead boats, and rusted-out tin advertising. A place where Dekkert had shot at me through a window and a brave little guy had taken a bullet meant for me, almost certainly saving my life.

No lights were on in the shanty, but in the moonlight you could see everything, the barrel of fish heads, the fishing poles leaning there like Huck and Tom just abandoned them, the ancient wheelbarrow—all forming a picturesque ivory-washed still life perfect for an artist inclined toward the rustic.

But something was missing.

What?

I circled the shack and on the other side saw a rumpled oil-stained tarp covering something. An awful chill went up my spine as my fingers grabbed the stiff fabric, and pulled it back, not knowing what the hell might be under there, expecting maybe little Poochie or, God help me, Velda.

A rowboat.

An old wooden wreck that had been salvaged but patched enough to most likely float, with a couple of ragged but usable oars.

I covered it up again.

The .45 was in my hand when I went through the unlocked makeshift door into the darkness of the shack. Enough moonlight came in to guide me around the homemade table and crates for chairs and over to the wall-mounted oil lamp, which I set a match to and flooded the room in an eerie orange glow.

No one here.

What had I expected to find? What answer did I think was waiting in this goddamn hovel? What nagging half-formed thought had sent me on this desperate, hopeless wild goose chase?

I prowled the little space, checking the single bunk and finding only the threadbare quilt and a couple skimpy, dirty blankets and a mattress with the thickness and consistency of a slice of burnt toast. The iron pipes of the stove were cold, though if someone had been here, it was cold enough tonight to have lit it. I went over everything, from the fireplace bin to the basin of scavenged utensils, and finally toured the collection of beautifully carved shells on the two-by-four shelving slung midway around three of the four leaning walls.

I sat on a crate at the little table and cursed myself. This was my fault, sending Velda out on her own, knowing a maniac was out there targeting beautiful women. I'd been in the city playing footsie with that minx Marion Ruston while Velda had been out there in the sticks in harm's way, and I would never forgive myself if anything happened to her, and if she *died*, if somebody *killed* her…

My eyes filled with tears and I wiped them away with my suit coat sleeve and as I blinked into focus, my vision fixed itself on the battered old cabinets beneath the shelving.

What was it Poochie had said about those fancy carved shells of his?

I got lots more. Down here is my private collection.

I went over and bent down. The cabinets were unlocked. Anybody could have strolled into that shack and cracked open those cabinets and seen what I saw. But no one ever had. Not that anyone would have believed it.

There on little pedestals carved out of driftwood was an array of intricately carved shells, the craftsmanship remarkable, the artistry incredible, like nothing I'd ever seen. And the subject matter, too, was like nothing I'd ever seen...

...two beautiful girls hanging by their heels from rafters with their bodies slashed, delicate paint-brush red touching each wound...

...a lovely girl spread-eagled in pornographic detail as she lay with wide eyes and bulging tongue and a nylon knotted around her throat...

...a lovely blonde similarly arrayed but on the edge of the beach, with the carving catching the curl of the waves half covering her body as she too stared upward with wide dead eyes...

...and that same blonde, Sharron Wesley again, the only subject who had rated two miniature masterpieces, slung over that statue of a horse with hair hanging like Lady Godiva and her once lush bottom in the air with pin pricks of the carver's artistry to indicate the decay.

And there were seven more scenes, seven other tableaus of murder, victims from somewhere, from who knew where, but all lovely young naked women, dead by murder, strangulation or the knife, in assorted grisly artistic variations.

On a bottom shelf was a sketchbook. I reached for it with a trembling hand. The cover was black and hard, like a library book, and it did not look new. This belonged to an artist who had used it for a while.

In that book were pencil drawings as skillful as they were horrific, scenes sketched at murder sites for the carver to take home and work from at his leisure. Some were not violent at all, rather scenes of victims taken from afar, as his subjects sat at outdoor cafes or went swimming or (framed in their bedroom windows) undressed. He had stalked his prey and prepared for his art, but for every exquisite carved shell of horror there were half a dozen sketches from various angles, capturing moments of stark terror in the faces of his "models."

And among the preliminary sketches of those models, among the life studies that the artist prepared before the death studies to come, were half a dozen sketches of Velda. In some she was with me (though my face was barely sketched, of no interest to this Michelangelo) as we ate, or strolled on the beach, or when she sunbathed alone or...

I slammed the book shut.

And when I opened the other cabinets, I was not surprised to find neatly stacked, an assortment of clothing of the type females like those coeds, Doris Wilson, and, yes, Sharron Wesley might have worn. But also the feminine clothing of seven other, as-yet-unidentified, victims.

Little Poochie the harmless. Little Poochie the victim. Little Poochie the beachcomber, the dimwit, the idiot savant.

Little Poochie the homicidal maniac!

I rushed out of the shack onto the beach and the moon was gone, clouds had drowned it, and nothing was left but a gray shadow-torn stretch of sand and an ocean whose raging waves were the color of gun metal, foaming like a rabid animal.

Where had the bastard taken her?

My eyes searched the outside of the shack for a clue. I understood the rowboat now—he had strangled Sharron Wesley, then stuffed her in his patch-up rowboat and gone out as far as he dared, which had not been far, and dumped her. Then when she washed up a week later—

on this same beach where he scavenged for shells and driftwood—he had taken the opportunity to create another artistic masterpiece using the same model. He had stuffed her bloated body, like the carcass of a mermaid flung to shore, into that old wheelbarrow and rolled her down the quiet, pre-season beach to where the park provided him with the perfect possibility for an artistic subject.

Lady Godiva by Stanley Cootz.

Goddamnit, if I'd only had the foresight to ask Pat to run a check, who knew what that name would have brought up?

But Poochie was too smart for me. He knew just how to hide. He created this moron persona and became a sort of invisible man.

How many beachfront communities had he drifted into, to take up residence in a shanty and play nonentity, while he stalked beautiful women and pursued his psychopathic art?

How many unsolved murders out there bearing his distinctive flourish of a signature would we discover in the aftermath?

But this was not the aftermath.

Right now we were very much in the midst of Poochie's grisly artistry. Somewhere *this minute* he was staging a ghastly tableau with Velda as his model, his subject, *and I didn't know where the hell he had taken her!*

Then I noticed it. The clouds slid by and revealed the moon and the moon revealed that thing that is the hardest of all to notice: an absence of something.

The cats.

Where were those sickly, scrawny cats? Those cats, one of which had torn my pant leg and the flesh beneath, were nowhere to be seen. They must have followed their master to the scene of his next artistic triumph.

And then I remembered: back at the Wesley place, those cats scrounging around those garbage cans; I'd seen them when I pulled into the drive and went after Dekkert. The mansion had been dark but the cats had been lingering around the edge of it, scavenging like their owner, waiting for him to finish.

I ran as fast as the sand would allow, skirting the dead boxer that had been mean to Poochie's cats, getting its neck broken like its mistress, and then cut up through the trees and toward the house, where dead men sunned themselves in the moonlight, and a safe full of money sat with its door yawned open and nobody giving a damn, the coppery scent of blood in the wind with a cordite chaser and the acrid after-stench of bodies that had soiled themselves as the sorry souls within had left this world.

The big colonial house loomed before me, a hulking dark shape like a crouched beast about to strike. No lights on. No sounds. Then the screech of one cat protesting the actions of another sent me scurrying closer, staying down, .45 tight in my fist. The felines were skulking around outside the garage now, fighting over the remains of some week-old bony half-eaten fish.

The garage door, I remembered, was the roll-type and it made a certain amount of noise. So I opened it slowly and eased it up just enough to throw myself under, rolling to a stop near the parked Cadillac. Sharron Wesley's fancy private ride.

I stayed silent, waiting for a reaction—a light to go on, a shot to be fired, a shout, anything.

Nothing.

I got up and leaned against the hood of the car and it was hot. As if I'd touched a stove, I brought my hand away, knowing that this vehicle had been recently driven, and noticing that it faced with its tail to the garage door.

And when I had seen it a few days ago, the Caddy's nose had been pointing that way.

Now a puzzle piece slid snugly into place. Chief Chasen at Wilcox had said of the two missing coeds: they had been seen *"piling into a fancy car…"*

And Poochie, the ragged little next-door neighbor in the shack down the beach, the nuisance who spent way too much time around the Wesley grounds, would be in a perfect position to keep track of the comings and goings of Sharron Wesley. Likely her trips to the city were in the company of Deputy Dekkert, and her "fancy car" had been left behind.

Sharron, remember, had a habit of leaving the keys in the glove compartment. That's where they'd been the other day and that's where they were now.

And Poochie could drive all right. Just because he was a "dimwit" beachcomber, that didn't mean he couldn't handle a vehicle. Hadn't he told me that he helped Sharron Wesley's party guests get their cars out of the sand, for tips? And that sometimes he wasn't strong enough to push, so he would get behind the wheel and *they* would push?

He sure as hell hadn't used his trusty wheelbarrow to haul Velda over here. He had grabbed her out of that phone booth, slugged her or chloroformed her or some goddamn thing, and brought her over in that Caddy, the very one sitting with its engine hot right now. All this after finally slipping out from under Doc Moody's watchful eye, faking his own kidnapping to explain his absence and throw more suspicion on Dekkert.

I slipped under the garage door and moved around the free-standing garage for another look at the house, gazing up at windows, checking for light, seeing only darkness. An artist, even as unique a one as Stanley Cootz, needed light to create his masterworks. I made a full circuit and was ready to say the hell with it, and just go in and take my chances, when I saw it.

At one end of the second floor, red light was bleeding from the windows of what I knew to be the ballroom. A deep red, a scarlet that recalled the lights the old-time prosties used to stick in their windows.

This trip I didn't bother with checking for the alarm device on the back door—if a loud blare sounded out, that was fine. It might spook the son of a bitch, and maybe spare Velda. If on the other hand the alarm was silent, and went off at the Sidon police station, for once I would be glad to see those sad sacks show up.

But Poochie had already unhooked the device—he really *did* know his way around the Wesley manse.

This time I didn't have a flashlight with me. But I remembered the lay-out well enough, and moved through the big kitchen and into the bigger casino room. A row of windows with the curtains back let in the moon reflecting off the choppy sea. You could hear the wind whistling and bitching as it tried to squeeze its way in, and shutters shook and trees rustled and the whole haunted house shebang might have rattled me, if I hadn't been so grateful for the moonlight. That made child's play out of maneuvering in and around the maze of craps and roulette tables.

Then I moved through the bar, which lacked windows to guide me, and knocked into a chair, scraping the floor. I froze, waited, watched, listened.

No response.

Nor could I hear any sound from upstairs. That might mean anything, including that Velda was dead already. If that was the case, Poochie would die one bloody inch at a time. I would find a knife and I would make a carving out of his sorry flesh that he could spend eternity envying in Hell.

Finally I found the hallway off of which were the front door, the cloakroom, and the stairway up to whatever madness was occurring up on the second floor. More moonlight came in from somewhere and let me see perhaps half of my way up the stairs, and when I reached the top, I could not see but could feel the thick Chinese rug under me, relishing how it muffled the sound as I moved down the corridor to that ballroom.

Its double doors were closed, but beneath them an edge of scarlet beckoned and pulsated—there was an almost liquid-like shimmer to it, as if a slaughterhouse on the other side had leaked its butchery under.

I opened the door slowly, cautiously, with my left hand on the knob, my right shoulder against the wood, the rod ready in my right fist. The door creaked, but I was in.

She hung upside-down on the stage, all the way down at the other end of the chamber, strung up naked by her ankles like the girls in that barn, swaying, swinging ever so gently, held up high enough that her bound wrists did not touch the flooring but her long locks flowed down behind her head to brush the stage while her beautiful, terrified, topsy-turvy face stared with wide eyes over a dirty rag of a gag. Stage lighting painted her and the entire tableau blood-red, turning the ebony of her hair scarlet, the signature of her sex a crimson pyramid, and as hideous as this humiliation was, Velda remained a beautiful creature, gravity failing to defeat the thrust of her breasts, the upended sweep of her body from the prominent ribcage to its narrow waist, from the jut of hips to the long, fully fleshed legs with their rope-bound ankles, making of her a sleek abstract shape, a flow of femininity that could not be made grotesque however evil the intent.

The rest of the ballroom glowed red as well, though not as intensely. Lights in the ceiling, caught by a mirrored, turning globe, flashed and reflected as if the room itself were blinking, as if this garish nightmare were shorting in and out, like a faulty circuit.

I didn't see him at first. The room seemed vast and empty. *Had he gone? Where was he?*

No matter. There was Velda to save.

"Velda!" I cried.

Did those wide eyes register that she had seen me, or was she in shock? Had this monster drugged her, and she didn't know what she was seeing? I couldn't tell, even as I ran and drew closer, if I was really getting a reaction.

But my cry did raise Poochie.

From the wings of the stage he emerged, his face a mask of confused interruption, but this was not the ragamuffin beachcomber I'd known, this was a different Poochie entirely.

This was a demon, small and red under the stage lights, an imp as naked as Velda, a hairless, bony, baby-bellied child man, with the under-developed, barely formed genitalia of an infant, his tiny member standing tall and defiant and pathetic.

Bare-ass and barefoot, the little red devil lacking only horns stood there with something other than a pitchfork in his hand—*what? Gun? Knife?*—glowering in dismayed shock as I barreled toward him.

Yet he had the presence of mind to fly to Velda, to crouch beside her, like an evil gnome, with his tiny sex dangling like unripe fruit with that little stem extended, and he held to her throat his carving knife, that shoemaker's blade he had used to fashion his intricate shells, and to slash those poor coeds hung by their ankles in that barn.

Like Velda.

And now the blade was dimpling the flesh next to Velda's throbbing jugular and her brown eyes were beacons of terror blazing into me.

I froze.

Poochie's smile was boyish. "Mike… Mike… you don't wanna make me kill the nice lady, do you?"

There was nothing different about his voice. Nothing new and demented to fit this evil dwarf, crouching there as if perched on Satan's armrest.

I had been wrong thinking Poochie had created a moron persona to hide behind. He was a moron all right, but a moron with a streak of obsession married to evil genius.

I paused at the edge of the stage, looking up at this obscene Halloween pageant. The .45 was in my hand. A head shot could take him out. That was my best bet—a head shot. His motor skills would shut off like I'd thrown a switch. But I could give him no indication of my intent.

Not with that blade so close to her jugular.

"I'm not a bad person, Mike… but I have desires… I have visions… dark ones. People think I'm stupid, but I have a *gift*, Mike. A gift to make the girls I choose seem real to me, and me to them… and then? Then I make them live forever! Don't you think so, Mike? Don't you think my work will be in a museum someday?"

"Poochie," I said, "I've been your friend. So has Velda. Just let her go."

His smile was gleeful, his eyes dancing with reflected red. "And you'll let *me* go? Or… get me *help*? But I don't want help, Mike! I like how I am. Most of the time, I don't bother people. I just go my way. I feed my cats and catch my fish and find my shells. I don't bother nobody. But when I get the feeling, the urge, I follow it. What's wrong with that? It seems right. It seems natural."

"It isn't, Poochie. You're sick. You're like a mad dog."

"What do they do to mad dogs, Mike? What do they do?"

In a moment I would cut Velda down. I would hold her and

comfort her, and take her out of this chamber of horrors, and we would gather that fortune waiting out there on the beach among the dead men, and she would laugh when I told her we wouldn't have to worry about me taking on so many cases for free anymore, not for a while anyway, and we would leave Sidon hand-in-hand and know better next time when somebody suggested a weekend away from dangerous New York City.

His upper lip was peeled back over his teeth and his eyes were crazy and dancing red. "I asked you a *question*, Mike! What do they *do* to mad dogs?"

I showed him.

ABOUT THE AUTHORS

MICKEY SPILLANE and **MAX ALLAN COLLINS** collaborated on numerous projects, including twelve anthologies, three films and the *Mike Danger* comic book series.

SPILLANE was the bestselling American mystery writer of the twentieth century. He introduced Mike Hammer in *I, the Jury* (1947), which sold in the millions, as did the six tough mysteries that soon followed. The controversial P.I. has been the subject of a radio show, comic strip, and two television series; numerous gritty movies have been made from Spillane novels, notably director Robert Aldrich's seminal film *noir*, *Kiss Me Deadly* (1955), and *The Girl Hunters* (1963), in which the writer played his famous hero.

COLLINS has earned an unprecedented sixteen Private Eye Writers of America "Shamus" nominations, winning for *True Detective* (1983) and *Stolen Away* (1993) in his Nathan

Heller series, which includes the recent *Bye Bye, Baby*. His graphic novel *Road to Perdition* is the basis of the Academy Award-winning film. A filmmaker in the Midwest, he has had half a dozen feature screenplays produced, including *The Last Lullaby* (2008), based on his innovative Quarry series. As "Barbara Allan," he and his wife Barbara write the Trash 'n' Treasures mystery series (recently *Antiques Disposal*).

Both Spillane (who died in 2006) and Collins are recipients of the Private Eye Writers of America life achievement award, the Eye.

AVAILABLE FROM HARD CASE CRIME

MICKEY SPILLANE & MAX ALLAN COLLINS

The Consummata
Dead Street

MAX ALLAN COLLINS

Two for the Money
Deadly Beloved
Seduction of the Innocent
The Last Quarry
The First Quarry
Quarry in the Middle
Quarry's Ex
The Wrong Quarry
Quarry's Choice

TITANBOOKS.COM

AVAILABLE FROM TITAN BOOKS

HELEN MACINNES

A series of slick espionage thrillers from the New York Times bestselling "Queen of Spy Writers."

Pray for a Brave Heart
Above Suspicion
Assignment in Brittany
North From Rome
Decision at Delphi
The Venetian Affair
The Salzburg Connection
Message from Málaga
While We Still Live
The Double Image
Neither Five Nor Three
Horizon
Snare of the Hunter
Agent in Place

TITANBOOKS.COM

PRAISE FOR HELEN MACINNES

"The queen of spy writers." *Sunday Express*

"Definitely in the top class." *Daily Mail*

"The hallmarks of a MacInnes novel of suspense are as individual and as clearly stamped as a Hitchcock thriller." *The New York Times*

"She can hang her cloak and dagger right up there with Eric Ambler and Graham Greene." *Newsweek*

"More class than most adventure writers accumulate in a lifetime." *Chicago Daily News*

"A sophisticated thriller. The story builds up to an exciting climax." *Times Literary Supplement*

"An atmosphere that is ready to explode with tension... a wonderfully readable book."
The New Yorker

TITANBOOKS.COM